---- ★ ----

THE SNAKES HAD COLD, BULGING EYES

Their silence was almost more frightening than their rattles. Tony and Pat seemed to hear each other's hearts.

In her soft, still-scared voice Pat said, "But I thought snakebites weren't fatal unless you were out in the wild—unless you couldn't get help for a couple of hours."

Tony nodded while slowly raising the bright blue duffel bag to chest height. "I've heard that, too." Now he held the bag under his chin with both hands. "It's an idea that I don't want to test. How 'bout you?"

After a pause she shook her head once. "No."

"Right. So I'm gonna toss this bag. Be ready to go— fast—and when you get inside, slam the door."

"But what about the *other* snake?"

"I think he's far enough away. I think he won't move if you're going away from him. How do *I* know! What do *I* know from snakes! All I know is what I read in the books! Don't argue and when I say go, go! And slam that door!"

The buzzing started again.

---- ★ ----

"It's not the Pratts' first b‍‍‍‍‍‍‍‍‍‍‍‍‍‍‍‍‍‍‍‍‍‍
hoped, won't be

Also available from Worldwide Mystery by
BERNIE LEE

MURDER AT MUSKET BEACH

MURDER
WITHOUT RESERVATION

BERNIE LEE

WORLDWIDE ®

TORONTO • NEW YORK • LONDON
AMSTERDAM • PARIS • SYDNEY • HAMBURG
STOCKHOLM • ATHENS • TOKYO • MILAN
MADRID • WARSAW • BUDAPEST • AUCKLAND

Dedicated to my mother, Beulah Kelly Lee.
And to my wife Helen, to our daughter Julia,
and to our son Dave.

MURDER WITHOUT RESERVATION

A Worldwide Mystery/May 1992

First published by Donald I. Fine, Inc.

ISBN 0-373-26096-2

Printed in U.S.A.

ACKNOWLEDGMENTS

Many thanks to Oregon State Police Sergeant Mike Searcey, Jefferson County Sheriff Mike Throop, Wasco County Sheriff Art Labrousse, and Chief Jeff Sanders and Lieutenant Bruce Fones of the Warm Springs Tribal Police; to Garland Brunoe of the Warm Springs Confederated Tribes, as well as to Robey Clark and Christine Landon; to Marjean Whitehouse of the Jefferson County Chamber of Commerce, and with special thanks to Patrick Eckford, Kiyoshi Nakamura, and Sho Dozono of Azumano Travel Service, and to Chiaki Matsushita of the Fuji Television Network.

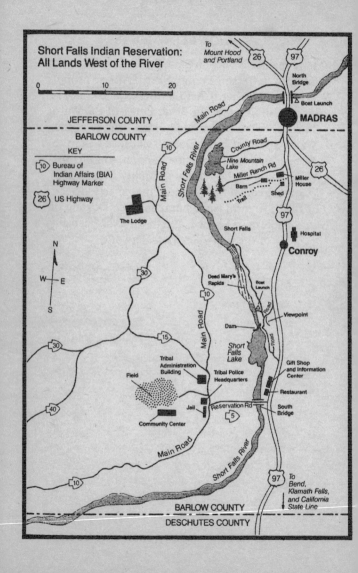

Short Falls Indian Reservation:
All Lands West of the River

0   10   20

JEFFERSON COUNTY

BARLOW COUNTY

KEY

10 Bureau of
    Indian Affairs (BIA)
    Highway Marker

26 US Highway

To Mount Hood and Portland

26 97

North Bridge

Boat Launch

MADRAS

Main Road

10

Short Falls River

County Road

Nine Mountain Lake

Miller Ranch Rd

Barn   Shed   Miller House

Trail

26

The Lodge

Short Falls

97

Hospital

Conroy

N
W   E
S

30

Dead Mary's Rapids

10

Boat Launch

Viewpoint

Dam

Road

Short Falls Lake

30

15

Tribal Administration Building

Field

Tribal Police Headquarters

Gift Shop and Information Center

Restaurant

30

Jail

40

Reservation Rd

5

South Bridge

Community Center

Main Road

Short Falls River

10

97

To Bend, Klamath Falls, and California State Line

BARLOW COUNTY

DESCHUTES COUNTY

PROLOGUE

TONY'S FIRST PROBLEM, before other problems nearly killed him and his wife Pat—before somebody shot the horse and the drug dealer, before Tony went crashing through white-water rapids to save a terrified nine-year-old boy from drowning, before the runaway grass fire, and before somebody dumped a pair of deadly rattlesnakes in their bedroom—before all of the other things that happened, Tony Pratt's first problem was to find a priest.

A Shinto priest.

Right here in the middle of Oregon's High Desert Country he was supposed to shuffle through the cattle ranchers, cowboys, loggers, and farmers and come up with a Shinto priest. To bless the Japanese TV crew.

Right.

Well. Nobody had told *him* about any Shinto priest! Not until almost dawn this morning.

There they'd been, Tony and all forty of the cast and crew, standing happily around the tripod-mounted video camera on top of that beautiful butte, looking out over mile after dark green mile of ponderosa pine toward the shadowy, snow-covered slopes of Mt. Jefferson, waiting for the sun to come up and light the first scene.

Slowly, the crew's cheery, nervous chattering had died away. Forty heads topped with shining black hair turned toward Tony. Forty pairs of solemn brown eyes stared at him. From under eighty raised eyebrows.

And out of that subdued crowd had come Nobutaka Okumura, from Kita TV in Tokyo, the producer and director. Nobu walked toward Tony, who was standing in front of the Ford Bronco, one boot up on the bumper.

Whenever he brought Tony a question or a problem Nobu always came straight on, firmly, but with his head bowed and his eyes looking down, then up to Tony past the worn, ragged bill of his Yomiuri Giants baseball cap. Then down. Then up again.

Tender and trim, Nobu walked through the dew-soaked sagebrush, the water turning his Levis even darker blue from the knees down, the spattering drops making spots in the red dust coating his white Nikes. Today's shooting schedule was on a clipboard in his left hand and he held it out from his side and up a little to keep the pages away from the spatters.

Nobu stopped and looked up from his five-foot-seven to Tony's almost-six-feet. "Tono-san," he said to Tony. His voice was quiet, a little sad, and surprisingly deep and big for his stature. He waved his clipboard in a short arc toward the people around the camera. "Tono-san. There is no priest."

Tony took his boot off the bumper and stood up straight. "Priest?"

Nobu ignored his troubles with the letters *r* and *l*. "Always," he said, "always—the number one thing—the first thing—a priest comes to bless the production. Always."

"No one told me."

"Not in my notes?"

"No."

"Hayashi did not say?"

"No one." Tony shook his head.

Nobu mirrored the head shake, slower. "We cannot begin without the blessing." His voice was soft and sad.

Tony looked at all the people looking back at him. He looked toward the little town of Conroy, half-an-hour east, then at the slowly brightening sky, then toward Portland, more than three hours west, and again at Nobu. "So important?"

"Essential."

He started toward the driver's side of the Bronco. "A Japanese priest?"

"That would be best. But..." Nobu flashed a quick smile, then shrugged.

Tony went on around to the driver's side. "I'll be back as soon as I can."

Now, a little more than an hour later, Tony laughed and shook his head. "How the hell did I get myself into *this* one?" He thumbed his sweaty straw Stetson off his forehead, wiggled into a fresh position behind the steering wheel, and laughed again.

How the hell did Tony Pratt, former partner in a successful San Francisco advertising agency, writer and producer of prize-winning television and radio advertising campaigns, now the author of four published mystery novels with another on the way—how'd he get *here*?

Here: Whipping a borrowed Ford Bronco down the narrow concrete strip of Central Oregon's Highway 97. Headed west across a summer-baked mesa spotted with isolated gray-green clumps of sagebrush. Catching glimpses of the tiny town of Conroy, the Barlow County Seat, getting even smaller in the rearview mirror. With a slight white-haired man in a black suit sitting beside him and gazing silently out the passenger side window, looking past the Bronco-made dust storms, past the sage and the few yellow blobs of rabbit brush, past an occasional gray-legged, gray-vaned windmill standing ankle-deep in dark green mintfields in the middle distance, looking out to the darker green stands of junipers clustered in the brown folds of the foothills below the snowy shoulders of the Cascade Mountains. An American priest preparing to offer a Latin blessing to a Japanese television crew.

That was the key, the TV crew. Three years earlier, a Portland travel agency had sold a Japanese TV company on shooting a series set in Oregon; with considerable political pressure from national, state, and local governments—and considerable financial support from national, state, and local businesses—the series was produced. "Norio In Oregon" showed the adventures of a nine-year-old boy named Norio, living with his mother on a farm in Central Oregon while his father teaches Japanese at a local university.

The show captured the hearts of the Japanese people. An immediate hit, it became a little like a Japanese version of "The Waltons" or "Little House on the Prairie"—an island of true family entertainment in the TV swamp of sex and violence. "Norio" became so popular that it drew an even bigger audience than Japan's World Series.

And the show's audience couldn't seem to get enough of it. The original series was renewed twice, and now the crew was back to shoot a "Movie of the Week" version.

Very few people in Japan had ever heard of the state of Oregon before the television show. Now, eighty percent of the Japanese knew about Oregon. And most of them wanted to come over and experience its size and sweep and endless natural beauty in person. Which was exactly what the travel agency, the governments, and the local businessmen had in mind.

Tony got involved through a friend of a friend connected with the state's tourism office. This shirt-tail friend knew his reputation as a television producer and recommended him to the Japanese to help with local casting, to scout locations, to contact local governments, and so on.

And so far, so good. That's how he got here. *But,* until an hour ago, nobody had told him that not one single foot of video tape would roll unless a priest gave his blessing.

And in the Pacific Northwest, Shinto priests are few and far between. About a hundred and sixty miles west-southwest, as a matter of fact. In Portland. Or maybe a hundred and eighty miles west-northwest, serving the few Japanese people among the apple and pear growers in Hood River.

Which brought on Tony's bright idea for the morning: Father James J. McCuddy of St. Michael's Church in Conroy. To Tony's Protestant eye—and perhaps to those of the Japanese, too, under the circumstances—a priest is a priest. And, he hoped, a blessing is a blessing.

Racing into Conroy, Tony'd found Father Mc-Cuddy standing in the street in front of St. Michael's, leaning sadly on a bag of golf clubs, staring down at the flat front tire on his Chevy Chevette. He'd met the slight, gray-haired priest before, at a Conroy Chamber of Commerce luncheon announcing the TV crew's arrival. Otherwise he'd never have recognized Father Mac dressed for an early-morning tee-off time in his Monday golf garb: lime polyester slacks, short-sleeve Madras shirt. Square on his head sat the kind of white

Panama hat with a round crown and turned-up brim that Charlie Chan wore in those old movies.

Tony stopped the Bronco nose to nose with the Chevy. He got out, walked around, and stood in the street beside Father McCuddy helping him stare at the tire.

"Flat as a cow pie," said the priest.

They communed over the flat for a few moments before Tony explained his own predicament and offered to trade favors.

"Thank you, but no," Father Mac said, "this is one of the reasons for joining the auto club." He tapped the tire with the toe of one of his white bucks as he let out a little laugh. "Say. Do you suppose I'm in the same line of work as *Triple A*? Road-side emergencies?"

Grunting, he hoisted the heavy golf bag up and slid the strap over his right shoulder. "Give me a couple of minutes. I'll telephone the Shell station and get somebody to come over to change the tire. Then I'll change me. Back into uniform." Starting toward his house he said, "If I can't play hooky, I'd better go to work."

AND THAT, Tony decided, is how he came to be wheeling this Bronco off narrow, two-lane U.S. Highway 97 and onto State Route 13, an even narrower blacktop. Two miles and a hard right turn later, its tires bit into gravelly Road 9 on the Short Falls Indian Reservation. After a mile and a quarter of spitting gravel it bumped onto the dusty track of Forest Service Road 46, rocked and bounced for three-quarters of a mile, and then stopped when the road stopped, suddenly, on the edge of a butte where Nobu and the crew waited as Tony had left them—looking out over miles and miles of ponderosa pine toward the snow-covered slopes of Mt. Jefferson, now glistening in the full morning sun.

Getting out of the car, Tony saw the scattered Japanese begin crowding together, like a congregation. Father Mac hopped out of the passenger side and unsnapped the small, battered old Gladstone bag he'd brought. There was a flurry of motion and color, mostly hidden by the high side and big door of the Bronco.

But in a few seconds, Father Mac slammed the door shut and walked around the front of the car. A swelling, sibilant murmur grew out of the smiling crowd of Japanese bowing, hands clasped, toward the priest striding slowly through the sagebrush in a flashing white alb. A brilliantly colored stole draped around his shoulders and down his sides. At his chest, and held gently with both hands, a silver aspergillum glinted with meaning in the sun.

Walking behind Father Mac, Tony took off his straw cowboy hat; in a rustling wave of motion the others took off their various baseball caps, straw hats, and leather sombreros.

The priest stopped in front of the crew. Tony motioned to Nobu to step forward. When Nobu and the priest were face-to-face, Tony introduced them: Nobutaka Okumura, noted producer and director, from the Kita Television Corporation in Tokyo, Japan; the Reverend Father James J. McCuddy, from the Church of St. Michael's, in the Roman Catholic Diocese of Conroy.

Tony moved back to stand beside the truck. For a few moments there was silence, except for the soft sound of wind rustling through the sage and the pines, carrying a sense of immense distance and space, the sound that's a constant presence in Oregon's High Country.

Father Mac, his white robe ruffling with the wind, moved his right hand in the sign of the cross. His voice came quiet, then rose strong and clear. And as he turned and raised his hands the folds of his robe opened like white wings toward the snow-covered mountain and his Latin prayer sang out over the pines and a golden eagle suddenly swept into view, soaring, then gliding across the mountain's white face, wings spread wide, riding up and away while the priest waved his silver aspergillum and punctuated his prayer with glittering rainbow sprays of holy water to the north, east, south, and west.

Nobu, head bowed, turned slightly, just enough movement to catch Tony's eye. He nodded once, slowly. He was pleased with Father Mac and his blessing. Which was good. But however good it was, it didn't stop somebody from shooting the horse and the drug dealer, didn't stop the robbery of the reservation's payroll, didn't prevent the runaway grass fire, didn't keep somebody from dumping a pair of deadly rattlesnakes in Tony and Pat's hotel room. In other words, despite the priest's wonderful blessing, all hell broke loose.

ONE

Monday

THE BRONCO was parked alongside the camera truck in the speckled shade of some pine trees, out of the hot August sun. The door on the driver's side was open to catch any bit of breeze drifting by. Tony Pratt sat sideways behind the steering wheel, boot heels hooked over the door frame. With his clipboard resting on his knees and a box lunch resting on the clipboard, Tony studied the shooting schedule while he finished another quick lunch.

Everybody else was having lunch, too—the forty-man crew and the four actors on call today. Sprawled in small groups on the blanket of pine needles in the spotty shade, they were enjoying a few minutes of rest from the hectic pace they had to keep up in order to finish a two-hour movie on time and on budget.

After three weeks of shooting, things were looking good. Not only had the dramatic sequences played well, but the scenic shots had been outstanding. Which was understandable, considering that they had all of Central Oregon to work with—beautiful rivers, rugged canyons, seemingly endless forests, sunny blue skies during the day and star-packed skies at night, and in the background the magnificently rugged snow-topped range of Cascade Mountains. And always, always this High Desert Country's sense of vast distance and space.

Now they headed into the last location week with only three major sequences left to shoot. Granted, they were the most dangerous scenes of all. Especially were they dangerous for the actors, and most especially for the little boy, Norio—the night scenes, where the nine-year-old is lost in the woods, the cattle drive and stampede, and the rafting sequence through white-water rapids. Knowing that every safety measure had been taken, however—and that every foreseeable problem had been worked out—Tony felt as sure as possible that nothing could go wrong in the few remaining days.

Finishing his lunch, he coaxed the last *M&M* out of its crinkled yellow sack. He dropped the sack in the empty lunch box. He put the box and clipboard on the floor. He pushed back and stretched out on the seat of the Bronco, boots out the doorway, hands under his head, straw Stetson over his nose, and settled in for an after-lunch doze till everybody else was ready to go.

A little later—half-asleep and half-awake, for how long he didn't know—the girl's pleading voice poked through his brief siesta.

Jo Miller was saying, "…and so anyway I talked to my dad and he said that Sunday would be fine, so…"

"But is it the proper thing, Miss?" Tony recognized the voice of Dennis Shimada, the handsome young Japanese actor.

"Are you so darned formal *all* the time? Is that a Japanese trait, or a custom in Japan?" She laughed a little. "Can't you just call me Jo?"

"All right." Shimada put a smile in his voice when he said, "Jo-san."

"Well, it's a start. And yes, having dinner at my house is proper."

Stretched out on the car seat, still drifting up out of a sleepy state, Tony heard leather creak, and a quick stutter of hooves; she'd swung up into her saddle. "And you'll *be* right here on the ranch to do that little scene, anyway. So when it's finished, we'll just go on to the house for dinner, then Dad or I will drive you back to The Lodge."

"I will ask Tono-san."

She started the horse walking away as she said, "All right, you ask Tono-san. I'm sure he'll say it's okay." Then, nudging her mare, she picked up the pace and called back over her shoulder, "See you later!"

The hoofbeats had barely begun to fade when a new, hard, high-pitched voice shook Tony wide awake. "Hold it, hero-san." The man's voice was rough and fast. "I thought I told you once before to stay away from her!"

"My name is Shimada, Mr. Hampton, as you know—Dennis Shimada."

"Your name is *nothin'* to me, Mr. hero-san. Now, I'm tellin' you for the *second* time and the *last* time: *Stay away from Jo Miller.* She's *mine.* I already kept a lotta better men than you away, and I ain't about to let some little Japanese TV hotshot move in."

"Please, can we discuss—"

"'Discuss' my ass! You just hear what I say. *Do* what I say. Or there's a good chance that you and Mount Fuji seen the last of each other!"

Heavy bootsteps pounded the ground. Then came the metallic creak-rattle-and-slam of an old car door. Tony eased his hat off and sat up slowly, just high enough to look over the dash and through the windshield and in time to see JayDee Hampton gun away in his punchdrunk yellow pickup. It flopped across the rocky ground so hard it almost bounced his rifle out of the gun rack across the rear window.

Before he skidded onto the dirt track of an old country road that ran down the western edge of Win Miller's land, Hampton hit the brake pedal once and the brake lights popped on. One was red and the other was white; the red plastic housing was broken off the right taillight. Then the whole truck disappeared in the dust as Hampton tore out for Miller's place, where he was foreman.

Another movement—closer—caught Tony's eye. Turning his head slightly, he focused on the mirror outside the Bronco's passenger window. At first, all he saw reflected there was the Japanese actor Dennis

Shimada, feet planted far apart in the dust, fists clenched at his sides, glaring down at the spot where JayDee Hampton had stood and threatened him.

Understanding Shimada's anger, Tony was about to look away when he realized what else it was in that reflection that had attracted his attention.

He focused on the mirror again. There he saw, barely visible in the background behind Shimada, peeking around the rear of the camera truck, the head and shoulders of Donna Hughes, the interpreter. She was frozen there as if in a state of shock, as if she herself had felt the full impact of JayDee Hampton's threat. Her left hand seemed to have grabbed at the front of her throat. Her right hand, as she stood behind him, was reaching out for Shimada.

TWO

Monday (continued)

By MID-AFTERNOON they'd wrapped up the day's principal shooting. Watching the actors climb into their van for the twenty-five mile drive back to the hotel, Tony Pratt remembered telling his wife, Pat, "The major problem on this job will be time. Time and distance. Central Oregon is so damned big that some days we'll be so far from what we want to shoot, hundred-mile round trips won't be unusual."

Today, it was only a fifty-mile round trip. For the actors. Tony still had a long way to go, driving Director Nobutaka Okumura and his cameraman and soundman to Nine Mountain Lake for another look at the location for tomorrow's shoot.

Now he stood by while Nobu gave detailed instructions to the assistant cameraman to shoot wild footage for use behind the movie's titles—isolated, unconnected scenes of surrounding mountains and forests, a nearby stream, and any other scenic shots that could serve as background while the credits were shown on the screen.

Finally the four of them—Tony and Nobu in front, cameraman and soundman in back—piled into the

Ford Bronco and went bouncing down a county road toward U.S. 97. Turning south on U.S. 97, they drove fifteen miles to the junction with State 114. Tony turned right on 114, driving west about a mile and a half where he pulled off the road and stopped in a long, narrow parking area beside a sign that said, "Viewpoint—Short Falls River Canyon."

When they hopped out of the Bronco their shoes crunched on coarse reddish gravel, scoria from the stubby dead volcano they were standing on. They walked across the parking area toward the edge of the canyon and stood behind a long knee-high fence made of peeled lengths of lodgepole pine.

Beyond the fence, the ground continued level about three more feet before it suddenly dropped away to the Short Falls River, two thousand feet straight down. Along the dim, shaded bottom of this narrow basalt cliff the river ran a deep dark blue with here and there a few flashing whitecaps.

Across the river and spreading out to the west, north, and south lay the Short Falls Indian Reservation, covering more than six-hundred-thousand acres. To the right, on reservation land, the canyon's west wall dropped away, sloping down almost to river level and letting the sun shine in. There the river narrowed sharply and sparkled in the sunlight, choppy water churning green and white for about three hundred yards—moderate Class One rapids, according to experienced river rafters. Then the Short Falls River flowed smooth and calm again for another hundred yards.

It was in those moderate rapids where the TV crew would shoot some of their remaining scenes, the sequence with the nine-year-old hero of the movie adrift in a rubber raft.

And it was in that calm hundred-yard stretch where they'd take him and his raft out of the water.

They had to get him out of the water there. A little farther on, the river turned vicious. Just below the quiet water, quickly and for almost a mile, the Short Falls River was a violent, foam-white killer, boiling and roaring over the hidden boulders and treacherous deadly suckholes of Dead Mary Rapids. Then it smoothed out for another quarter-mile before crashing down the short, shallow falls that gave it its name. Not even the experts rafted Dead Mary Rapids; here they portaged or lined their boats around to safer water.

Upriver, to the left, the riverbed was wider. There the water flowed slow and serene, like molten silver under the hot August sun. And above *that* mile-long stretch stood the tall, concrete face of Short Falls Dam, controlling the river's flow.

Behind the dam lay Nine Mountain Lake, a reservoir and water playground for Central Oregon's dry and thirsty High Desert Country.

And standing above it all were the rugged Cascade Mountains, tall and topped with snow or dotted with eternal glaciers, their nine major peaks ranging north and south as far as the eye could see.

Tony and the three Japanese spent several moments in silent admiration before Nobu noticed several small plaques attached to the low fence guarding the canyon rim. They said, "Beware of Snakes."

Nobutaka pointed to the little sign and looked at Tony. "This is true?"

Tony nodded. "Yes, I'm afraid so."

Something in Nobu's voice caught the cameraman's attention. He, too, pointed to the sign, saying something in Japanese to Nobu.

Nobu, apparently, translated "Beware of Snakes" into Japanese for the cameraman and the soundman. Instantly, their eyes seemed to pop out about three inches.

They began searching the barren ground all around, where nothing but fenceposts and gravel grew. At the same time they grunted short, sharp words at Nobu. And Nobu asked Tony a series of short, sharp questions, translating the answers just as quickly into Japanese.

"What kind of snakes?"

"Rattlesnakes."

"Poison snakes?"

"Yes."

"Here?"

"Yes."

"Dangerous?"

"Yes, when they shed their skin, especially. When they shed their skin they lose their eyelids. They get very irritable. Very nervous."

"Nervous?"

"Very."

"They bite? They strike?"

"At anything that comes close."

"This happens when they shed their skin?"

"Yes."

"When do they shed their skin?"

"Some time during the summer. July. August."

"Now the time is August?"

"Yes."

Tony barely saw them move. As he told Pat later, he was aware only of the fast patter of feet crunching on gravel, three little trails of dust puffs across the parking lot, and doors banging shut on the Bronco.

THEY DROVE THE SLOW, switchback country road down to the river where they reviewed their plans for shooting the rafting sequence, and after that they climbed back up the switchbacks and drove on to Nine Mountain Lake, to confirm the sites for tomorrow's shoot. Then, in the fading summer afternoon, Tony started the Bronco on the long drive back toward Conroy and on to their hotel.

In the rearview mirror he could see the cameraman and soundman, each curled into a corner of the back seat. Like the rest of the crew, they took every opportunity to grab a few minutes' sleep, trying to make up for the long, long days and short nights.

He glanced over at Nobu, who was, as usual, making notes to himself on his schedule.

"I want to tell you about something that happened this afternoon," Tony said quietly.

"Yes?" Nobu continued writing.

"We may have a couple of problems."

"Ah." Nobu clicked his ballpoint pen and turned to Tony. "Yes?"

"You know Jo Miller. The blonde girl?"

"Of course. Her ranch—her father's ranch—is the one we rent for many scenes. We also pay to use his cattle for the cattle drive. Yes. And you ask about her for what reason?"

"Because she seems to be infatuated with one of your actors."

"Excuse me?" Nobu glanced at Tony and flashed a smile, quick and bright, before settling his face in a questioning frown. "'Infatuated'?"

"She may think she's falling in love with one of the actors, Dennis Shimada."

"Ah. 'Infatuated.' I see." To himself, softly but aloud, Nobu added, "A new development." He turned and looked out the window.

The sun slipped a little lower behind the mountains. The wide blue sky became a little deeper blue. A few of the brightest stars began to sparkle. Trails of gauzy white cirrus clouds changed slowly into drifting scrims of soft vermilion.

Tony switched the headlights on and the beams shot out and put a shine on the broken yellow line down the middle of the cracked blacktop. Behind the fenceposts along the roadside, shadows jumped up and raced away in the opposite direction.

"And there's another new development that goes with the first one. JayDee Hampton."

"The cowboy?"

"Right. Works on the Miller ranch."

Nobu sat back and let his head relax against the top of the seat, waiting for Tony to tell the rest.

"As I said, Jo Miller is showing interest in Shimada—"

"Yes?"

"—but if *he* shows any interest in *her,* Hampton has threatened Shimada."

Nobu groaned and said, "Oooh, why now? First, Dennis and the interpreter. Now this. And so near to being finished. What should I do, sew his pants shut? A few more days, only, and we would be on the way home. Why should these things happen now?" He sat up again, tapping the tip of his pen on the clipboard.

"Well, nothing's happened between Jo and Shimada yet. And it'll probably stay that way if we just keep those three away from each other till we finish shooting and the show's all wrapped up. That, after all, is the most important thing."

Nobu nodded. "True. The work is important. At the same time, if two people want to be together, is it for me to say no?—to tell Shimada to stop?—to not talk to this girl?" Now he shook his head. "No."

"I'm not sure that would be as difficult as you think. From what I heard, Shimada didn't sound as though he wanted to get involved."

"Yes?"

"I think so." Tony shot a quick glance at Nobu before going on. "My main concern is Hampton. If that cowboy picks a fight with him, Shimada may get hurt. And if Shimada gets hurt now, what happens to the show?—he's very important in some of these final scenes."

"Hmmm," Nobu said.

"Right."

For a few minutes the only sound came from the tires humming on the blacktop, with an occasional hiss when they passed through a patch of asphalt still soft from the day's ninety-plus heat. On the road ahead, the tall shadowy shape of the grain elevator outside Conroy appeared in the distance. A few lights twinkled on the edge of town.

"My suggestion is that you, as director and producer, tell Shimada—*suggest* to Shimada—that his attitude toward Jo Miller should be polite but distant."

"Distant?"

"Be polite, but cool."

"I see."

"Decline all invitations, politely. Say that he has to rehearse. Or he has to rest to be ready for shooting. Anything. Or, if you don't want to tell him how to handle it, you could actually keep him so busy that he won't have time to get involved."

"I agree with your second suggestion."

"Good. And I'll talk to Jo. Explain how tight the rest of the shooting schedule is, tell her we can't afford any distractions for the next few days." Tony paused and then went on, "To tell you the truth, though, if anybody causes a problem, I don't think it'll be Jo Miller *or* Dennis Shimada. It'll be JayDee Hampton."

"Why do you think so?"

"Just a feeling." Tony glanced at Nobu again. "Ever meet anybody like that? When he comes around, you just *feel* something bad in the air—"

"Ah ha—"

"—you can almost *smell* it."

"—yes, I know the feeling."

"The guy is trouble."

Their voices had finally roused the two in the back seat. The cameraman and the soundman leaned forward, the cameraman asking Nobu a question.

Tony, guessing, asked him another. "They want to know what we're talking about?"

"Yes." A quick back-and-forth in Japanese followed, ending with the cameraman and soundman sitting back again, nodding and laughing.

"Sounds like a happy solution," Tony said.

Grinning, Nobu said, "They say, 'Leave Shimada on his own—actors always think they can do better without the crew.'"

Tony laughed. "That sounds like something a cameraman might say."

Nobu's expression turned serious. "Then they say, 'If the cowboy makes trouble, remember: there is one cowboy but forty crew.'"

"Are you joking?"

Nobu shook his head. "They laugh, but they are serious."

"Wonderful," Tony said sarcastically. "The perfect solution. A gang fight. Then Hampton goes and gets some more cowboys, and the first thing you know we've got a war on our hands."

BUT THE DAY ENDED on a good note for Tony, when he made his nightly phone call to Pat at their home in Lakewood, a Portland suburb. Her financial consulting business, usually slow during the summer, had been surprisingly busy. Now, though, it seemed to be tapering off.

"So," she said, "if you can spare some time for me, I'll try to get away Thursday for a long weekend."

"What do you mean, 'If you can spare some time'?"

"Well, you're down to the last week or so of shooting, aren't you?—from what you've said in the past, that's usually when it gets to be the most frantic."

"There's *always* time for a wife or two."

"If you're busy, though, I suppose I can always laze away by the pool."

"Not in this desert sun!—you'd burn to a crisp."

"Might burn off a few pounds."

"You don't need to lose any weight—"

"Well, aren't you nice."

"—but if you think so, I know a great horizontal exercise."

"You've been away too long."

"You're telling *me*!"

THREE

Tuesday

AT TWENTY MINUTES till seven Tony finished his second cup of coffee, signed his name and room number on his breakfast check, picked up his briefcase, and walked out of the dining room of the Short Falls Indian Lodge. Smiling to himself, he was looking forward to introducing Pat to Indian fry bread.

From the dining room he walked through the lobby past leather-slung chairs and a big octagonal, gray stone fireplace that crouched under a gleaming copper hood, past the desk where he dropped off his room key, and on to the Lodge's main entry. He pushed the wide carved-cedar double doors open and stepped out on the broad veranda that banded two sides of the arrow-head-shaped hotel. There he stopped and stood for a few minutes to watch a new day coming to Central Oregon, to tabletop buttes standing on tall basalt columns, to rolling hills speckled with sage and juniper, to deep slab-sided canyons and coulees dark with morning shadow, to lordly white-crowned mountains.

The three-story Lodge rode on a wide, flat-topped ridge whose flank sloped down to the Short Falls

River. A thin morning mist, rising from the river, drifted up the slope. Flat, early light filtered through the mist and laid long morning shadows in the deep draws and behind the trees and sagebrush clumps, the hills and outbuildings.

Looking at it now, he regretted that he'd never brought Pat and their kids to this resort on the Short Hills Indian Reservation. Since moving from San Francisco fourteen years ago, they'd explored and enjoyed Oregon's wondrous variety—from the Coast Range to Astoria on the northwest corner and all the way down the coastline to the Rogue River next door to California—to Ashland's Shakespeare Festival in the soft, rolling foothills of the Siskiyou Mountains—to the northeast corner and the Wallowa Mountains, or "America's Alps" as the locals say. And now with Jenny and Dan growing up, the whole family had seen a lot more of the Willamette Valley—especially the college towns of Eugene and Corvallis.

And in all that time, not one of their rafting or skiing or camping or exploring trips had included time here on the Short Falls Indian Reservation, except to speed across it on Highway 26 going someplace else.

But there was a lot to see and do here, even in this comparatively small area that was open to non-Indians. Looking down from the Lodge veranda Tony saw the first few holes of the eighteen-hole golf course, stretched along the bluff above the Short Falls River and sheltered by dogwood trees, willows, and Spanish olives.

To the right of the golf course the bluff slanted down to river level and there was a boat launch where hotel guests rented canoes and rafts. To the right of that ranged the dark green barns and white corrals of a riding stable from which the faint, thin thread of a trail led up and over the ridge the hotel rested on. Past the hotel, the trail faded away through a half mile of dry grass and sagebrush till it disappeared in the cool, deep green forest on the slopes beyond.

To Tony's left were covered tennis courts—covered for protection from the sun. And a swimming pool sparkled between the hotel's two wings in the cool shade of a poplar grove.

Smiling to himself again, thinking about seeing Pat again and showing her around, Tony crossed the parking lot and climbed into the Bronco.

He took the narrow access road that snaked down from The Lodge a quarter of a mile and connected at a T-intersection with the reservation's main road. A left turn would lead him ten miles to one of two bridges that crossed the Short Falls River from the reservation to U.S. 97. Instead, he turned right on Reservation Main and drove twelve miles to the Administration Center of the Short Falls Indian Reservation. Here, at a four-way intersection, ran the other road that spanned the river, linking the reservation to the highway.

Set back from each corner of the intersection was a grove of tall willow trees, planted so that their wide round crowns brought day-long shade to the one-story white stucco buildings tucked below. The tribal administration staff worked in the largest of the four buildings. The other three housed Jeff Nathan's General Store, the reservation fire department, and the tribal police, whose day shift was just going on duty as Tony pulled in. He drove on slowly for a few yards and parked in front of the jail. He pulled a file folder out of his briefcase and walked back along the edge of the parking strip toward the headquarters front door.

There stood five or six uniformed officers in sharply creased, short-sleeved khaki uniforms. All were above average height. One was straight and slim. The others had the broad, thick-shouldered torso and narrow hips so common in this tribe's males.

Hatless, their black hair shining and catching stray rays of the morning sun, they clustered around three dusty green Ford sedans and an even dustier Jeep. A standard light bar spanned the roof of each Ford, but the red-and-blue emergency lights were almost buried beneath a cake of red-gray dust.

And a thin sheet of dust seemed to drape around the front door of every car, including the Jeep, so that Tony could just barely make out the tribal police insignia on the doors. It was a circle of sage green ringed with a thin red line. Laid over the green was a gold block representing the shape of the reservation,

roughly rectangular. Gold letters within the top arc of
the circle said "Short Falls" and in the bottom arc
"Tribal Police." Each officer wore a version of the
same insignia on a shoulder patch on his left sleeve.

As Tony walked by, one of the policemen said,
"The guy that works for Win Miller?—that's the one
you're talking about?" Another one said, "Same
guy." Which made the first officer shake his head and
say, "What a temper. Some day he's gonna talk too
strong too long and to the wrong man."

Tony paused with his hand on the front door hoping to hear more but the conversation didn't pick right
up so he pushed on through the swinging doors.

Inside police headquarters he walked across the
square of worn gray linoleum in the small lobby area
toward a dark-haired girl behind the reception desk,
which was set in a tall, narrow opening cut into the
wall. There was a closed, windowless door to the left
of her desk.

She looked up and smiled a quick smile. "Good
morning."

"Good morning. I have an appointment to see
Chief Moody."

"Okay, just a second." She pushed an intercom
button and said, "Dad?"

Her intercom speaker erupted in a burst of static
with a deep voice inside it. "Yah."

"*A man's* here." She put a slight, odd inflection on the first two syllables. "Says he's got an appointment."

After another burst of static—"Okay, be there in a minute"—she took her finger off the intercom and flashed her on again-off again smile at Tony. "Get that?"

"He'll be here in a minute."

"Right."

She turned back to her Selectric. On the wall above hung a map of Oregon, mostly green, with a red line defining the reservation, mostly brown. The girl saw Tony studying the map and said, "Right. Our people got moved from over by the Columbia River and all that water over here to almost a desert. Guess it shows that people can get used to almost anything." She tossed her head, shrugged, and went back to work.

Tony looked beyond her at the others working behind littered desks in the busy, crowded office. Women of various shapes and sizes, all wearing T-shirts and slacks, they talked on the phone, typed, or shoved papers into folders and filed them away. The only difference between this and any other office was that each of these women had a tiny pointed party hat on her head. Scanning the room again, Tony spotted a semibare tabletop in front of a corner window. Spread out on the table were several paper coffee cups, a Mr. Coffee machine, and the remains of a large chocolate cake with vanilla frosting.

A door opened in the other corner of the office framing a short, round man in civilian clothes, brown shoes, brown pants, yellow shirt, tan tie. "'lizabeth," he called across the room. His voice was almost as gravelly as the static on his intercom.

The girl turned her head to him. He raised a fist and pushed out a thumb. She turned back, pressed a button on the corner of her desk, and a buzz rattled the knob on the door by her desk. She nodded at Tony and he pushed the door open and walked on through.

Making his way past a woman at one of the desks, he motioned toward her party hat and winked at the police chief. Moody nodded, holding out his hand, and as he and Tony shook hands he said, "I have a reputation for not running a taut ship, as they say in the Navy." They broke off the handshake and he motioned Tony on into his office. "But the way I look at it, if people are gonna have office birthday parties, do it in the morning. First thing. Get it out of the way and get to work. Otherwise they look forward to it all morning and then talk about it all afternoon and their minds are not really on the job. This way, it's over early and they can get something done. Want a piece o' cake?"

"No, thanks, Chief."

Moody walked around his desk and stood there kneading the back of his upholstered chair. He looked at Tony. "Feels kinda funny, doesn't it?"

"What's that?"

"Calling an Indian 'Chief'?"

Tony started to smile but before he could say anything Moody said, "I always like to get that one out of the way right away." He waved a stubby hand. "Just call me Jess."

Moody sat down and swiveled into position behind his desk, waving Tony to one of the chairs on the other side at the same time that he plucked the top note from a stack on his desk. "And your name is Tony Pratt?—working with this Japanese TV crew that's running all over the countryside?"

Tony nodded his head and said, "And the reason I called for an appointment this morning is to talk to you about clearance for some shooting we want to do on the river."

"Sounds like you want to talk to the Tribal Council. They're the ones who decide about non-Indians using anything on the reservation—roads, land, rivers, whatever."

"Right," Tony said. He lifted a letter out of his folder and handed it across to the chief. "I wrote to the Tribal Council and got this letter giving us permission to use the river on Tuesday, a week from today. But we might want to do it Monday. Or maybe even sooner."

"That's fine with us." Moody handed the letter back. "Except for Monday. On Mondays we're short-handed because one of our guys makes the money run.

So we won't have anybody to keep you folks out of trouble.''

Tony started a smile. ''Well, I don't think we need a *chaperone* to——''

Chief Moody raised a hand, palm out in a gesture that said, ''That's how it is. Don't argue.'' He dropped his hand back on his desk. ''When that many people come on the reservation, they get a chaperone. Rules of the road.''

''Okay.''

''Anything can happen. You never know.''

Tony shrugged.

''So I always put one of our officers with a group like that. You never know. But, as I said, we'll be short-handed. Gonna be short-handed *anyway* 'cause the crowds are startin' to show up for Reservation Days this weekend. Which means the guy making the money run is gonna be loaded.''

''What's this 'money run'?''

''Every Monday morning one of our police officers goes to The Lodge, and the restaurant and gift shop over at the highway junction—they're all run by the tribe. He collects the weekend receipts and takes the money and checks and stuff to the bank in Conroy.''

''Must be quite a haul.''

''Some days it is.'' The chief pushed back from his desk and stood up. Tony stood, too. ''Well. As I said, it's alright with us if you change the day you use the river, just so you let us know what you decide on, and just so it isn't Monday. But you *still* should go see the Tribal Council. Let them know."

"But they just meet on Monday, Wednesday, and Friday, don't they?"

"Not this week. With Reservation Days coming up they're meeting every day." He looked at his watch. "They oughta be in session right now, in fact. At the Administration Building right across the road."

"Okay, I'll go over and try to see the Council this morning."

"Here, let me have that letter again," Moody said. Tony gave it to him and he bent down and wrote a quick note across the bottom of the page. "Maybe it'll help if they know you're covered here." Handing the letter back, Moody added, "And I'll call over there and tell 'em you're coming. Might help." He shrugged. "You never know."

"Thanks." Tony held out his hand. "And thanks for your time."

Shaking hands again, the chief said, "Good luck."

Tony stopped in the doorway and turned back. "By the way, that's a good-looking shoulder patch your officers wear."

Moody nodded, then there was about a half-second pause before he said, "The old one or the new one?"

"Gold outline of the reservation on a green field? Gold letters? Inside a red circle."

"Oh, yeah. That's the old one." Moody nodded and reached for his telephone.

"What's the new one?"

The chief looked at Tony with a straight face and then started dialing. "Wagon train on fire. Inside a circle of Indians."

AN HOUR LATER, Tony and a young couple walked cheerfully out of the reservation's Administration Building. Tony had his schedule change approved, and the couple had to pass to pick up a runaway raft on the reservation side of the river.

Talking as they walked down the hall and left the building, Tony discovered that they ran a fishing guide service out of Bend, a town a few miles south of Conroy. Camped beside the Short Hills River the night before, one of their customers had let a fourteen-foot rubber raft get away and it washed up on the reservation shore about a quarter-mile below The Lodge.

"How's the water above Dead Mary Rapids?" Tony asked. "Looks sort of low."

"It's always low at this time of year," the man said, "easy to get through." He looked at his wife. "Right?"

"No problem," she said to Tony. "But I understand they're gonna release water over the dam sometime soon, and if you're in the rapids when it happens they could be really treacherous."

"Thanks for the tip," he said, "we'll check it out." They stopped beside a wrinkled-looking Volkswagen van. At that moment Tony glanced over toward the police station and saw one of the tribal officers coming out of the door to the jail. "And good luck in getting your boat out." He left the couple climbing into their van and trotted across Reservation Main toward the jail, where he'd parked the Bronco.

He waved at the officer who stopped in front of the Bronco, waiting, watching Tony hurrying toward him. When Tony got there he introduced himself, explained that he was working with the Japanese TV crew, and asked about the officer's comment that he'd overheard earlier.

"You were talking about a guy who works for Win Miller. You mean JayDee Hampton?"

"That's the guy."

"Can you tell me what happened?"

"Nothing 'happened.' The way I hear it, he was just standing in the middle of a crowded bar tellin' the world that he was takin' bets that some Japanese actor would never get out of Barlow County alive."

Tony shook his head. "Nice guy."

The officer just looked at him, deadpan. "Typical. Anything else?"

"No. Thanks."

The officer ducked his head once, turned, and walked on to the main door and went through it. Tony got into his Bronco, crossed Reservation Main, and drove on toward the bridge to Highway 97, wondering about ways to keep JayDee Hampton away from

the crew—and away from Dennis Shimada in partic-
ular—during the few days they had left in Oregon.

They needed JayDee, or someone like him, to handle the cattle for scenes where they were involved.
They needed him most definitely for shooting the
stampede. And at this point, trying to find someone
to replace him would take a good deal of trouble and
too much time.

Mulling on possibilities, Tony braked at the stop
sign under the flashing yellow light that marked the
intersection with Highway 97. He turned right, rolling past the Short Hills Reservation Gift Shop on the
corner. A little farther on was the restaurant. Between them was a shared parking lot. A few truckers,
tourists, and other travelers pulled in, pulled out,
shuffled in, shuffled out, or leaned back against the
side of the car reading a road map.

In the middle of the lot glittered a shiny new
Cadillac convertible, fire engine red, top down. The
pale, slick-haired driver was tall and thin so that his
skinny shoulders hit high on the seat-back and his
narrow, glossy head almost topped the windshield. He
had parked driver's window to driver's window beside an old pickup with its right rear taillight knocked
out.

Just as Tony drove by and began accelerating to
highway speed, he saw JayDee Hampton lean out the
truck window and drop something in the slick-haired
man's lap.

FOUR

Wednesday

WATCHING THE ACTION in front of The Short Falls
Lodge early the next morning was like tuning in a re-
run: The television cast and crew had played the same
scene at five-thirty each morning since they'd started
shooting. Tony missed it yesterday because of his appointment with the tribal police. Now he stood by the
front door looking at semi-organized chaos.

Sleepy-faced actors, actresses, and crew members
rushed and stumbled out of The Lodge, finishing
breakfast on the run, slurping coffee from thermos
tops and plastic cups, munching doughnuts or toast or
bacon and eggs. The bus, van, and equipment truck
sat rumbling quietly, their doors hanging open. A
couple of kitchen workers tried to push quickly
through the crowd with box lunches stacked high on
wheeled carts. The cameraman, soundman, and their
assistants came at a fast waddle under their load of
cameras, lens cases, and remote recording equipment, which they took to their rooms every night,
never leaving their gear overnight in the truck.

Nobu Okumura and his two assistant directors
darted in and out of the melee, circled its edges,

checked lists, waved their clipboards, trying to maintain some sort of order, hurry things along, and at the
same time keep everything as quiet as possible out of
consideration for the other hotel guests who were still
trying to sleep.

Watching all this, Tony was surprised to see an
added starter move into the action—a white Oregon
State Police cruiser had turned off the access road and
was inching through the crowd toward the veranda.

After a few moments of seeing sleepy people stum-
ble past and all but crawl across the hood of his car,
the driver found a quiet way to wake everybody up. He
reached over and snapped on his flashing, whirling
overhead lights. A path cleared immediately. The car
rolled ahead and stopped by the veranda steps where
Tony was standing.

When the officer opened his door and got out, Tony
had the feeling he'd seen him before—tall, trim,
square jaw, thin lips, narrowed eyes. "Good morning," the officer said across the roof of his car.

"Good morning," Tony said. "You're up early."

"Still up." Walking around in front of his car the
officer said, "You're Mr. Pratt, right?"

"Right." Tony recognized the cool gray eyes and the
flat voice. He also recognized the look and sound of a
man who was not happy in his work. "And you're
Trooper Kelsey."

"It's 'Sergeant,' now. 'Sergeant' Kelsey."

"Ah. Excuse me. Sergeant. I didn't see the stripes. But we met over at the coast, didn't we? At Musket Beach?"

"That's right. I cooperated with Officer Barrett of the Musket Beach Police. Investigating a problem you were involved in. On the beach and then at the home of an actor, as I recall."

"You get around."

"Things happen—promotions, transfers. You know how it goes." By this time Kelsey had moved up the steps to stand beside Tony. His eyes roamed over the people milling around the various vehicles before he asked, "So you're the contact with this TV crew?"

"Right," Tony said, and then corrected himself as he pointed to Nobu. "But the fellow who's *really* in charge is the one in the black baseball cap—Nobu Okumura. But if he's busy or not around, you can talk to me and I can take any questions."

"Okay."

"And you're our caretaker for the day?"

Kelsey shrugged. "Everybody in the Bend stations is sharing the load of watching out for these folks. But I've been tied up on some other business and missed my share till now, so—yep—today's my turn in the barrel."

"That's a great way to put it."

"That's about the way it is," Kelsey said. He shook his head. "Everybody's got his eye on this outfit, from the governor on down. The word is that these guys and their TV shows over *there* make a real impact on the economy over *here*. Somehow.''

''So I've heard. 'Very effective promotion for the state,' they say.''

Nobu was herding the last of the crew into the bus. The doors closed on the actors' van and the equipment truck.

Kelsey said, ''The airlines, the hotels, supposedly the whole tourist business likes what these people are doing. So we're supposed to keep 'em out of trouble, see that nothing happens to 'em. In fact, if there's anything we can do to help, we're supposed to drop everything and do it.'' He shook his head again.

''You don't seem to think much of the idea.''

Kelsey's gray eyes studied Tony before he said, ''Orders are orders. And we'll do what we have to do. But most of us didn't go into law enforcement so we could play nursemaid to a bunch of actors. Not with everything else that's goin' down right now.''

''What do you mean?''

The gray eyes glanced at Tony again. ''Cops in the country are facing the same problems as cops in the city, Mr. Pratt. Including drugs.''

He paused, looking up and out across the river to the hills and the taller buttes and on to the mountains. ''Even 'way out here in the boonies we got druggers and pushers and the whole shit-a-ree. Maybe not as many as in the city. But we don't have as many cops, either. And we've got one whole helluva lot more ground to cover."

The equipment truck ground into gear, cutting off conversation. Both men watched it move across the parking lot, trailed by the actors' van. The crew bus idled, door still open, and Nobu was hurrying across the lot toward Tony.

"So," Tony said, picking up his conversation with Kelsey, "what can you do about it?"

"So we'll keep after the bad guys as hard as we can go, the way we've been doing. But we'll also do what we can to help these people, too. Just makes it a little harder, is all."

Nobu arrived at the veranda. Standing a step below Tony and Kelsey, he flashed a half-second smile and said quickly, "Excuse, please, Tono-san. Shimada and Donna are not yet here. You will bring them when you come?"

"Yes. Sure. I'll call their rooms and shake 'em up. But have you met Sergeant Kelsey?"

After Tony's fast, informal introduction Kelsey said to Nobu, "So you're the man in charge here?"

Nobu nodded once, almost a half-bow, grinning a wide white grin. "Sometimes yes, sometimes no. Sometimes my job is producer, sometimes director." He laughed as he spoke, and his words seemed to come bouncing out on little spurts of air. "Sometimes my job is room clerk, sometimes baggage man." There were understanding chuckles and nods from the others, but then Nobu frowned at the hotel's front door. "Now I am—how do you say—bus dispatcher." To Tony he added, "This is not customary for Shimada, to be late."

"I know. You go ahead with the crew. I'll call upstairs right now."

"Good." Nobu started to say something to Sergeant Kelsey but instead turned back to Tony. "Do you notice the scent in the air?—smoke?"

Kelsey answered him. "That's just a slash burn, couple of miles west of here. Should be out by tonight."

Nobu's quick smile flashed while he said, "I'm sorry—'slash burn'? This is new to me."

The trooper waved a thumb over his shoulder. "Some loggers are working a couple of ridges back of here. What they trim off the logs is called 'slash' and they burn it before pull-out."

Nobu grinned again and his head tilted back. "Ah. I see. Thank you." From across the parking lot came a loud revving roar from the engine of the crew bus and Nobu hurriedly held his hand out to the sergeant. "Please. My apologies, but I must go."

"No problem." For the first time since Tony had known him, Kelsey's thin straight mouth moved in what might have been a smile. "Don't miss your bus."

Nobu bobbed his head once and ran back to the bus and hopped in.

"Busy man," Kelsey said.

"Hard worker, too," Tony said. "And good to work with."

The crew bus headed down the access road while Tony told Sergeant Kelsey where they'd be shooting for the next few days, then Kelsey got into his car and drove off.

Tony started toward The Lodge door but at that moment Dennis Shimada came bursting through. He rushed out and stood on the veranda frowning in the direction of the disappearing bus. Donna Hughes, the interpreter, walked calmly through the door behind him, smiling a slow smile.

She turned her smile on Tony. "I told him there was no need to hurry," she said. "I knew you'd be here. Or somebody." Looking again at the handsome Japanese actor she said, "But he became so impatient."

Shimada spun around, frowning now at Donna, and when he spoke Tony was impressed once more by the strength and authority he projected in his voice. It was a well-trained actor's voice, not deep but full, with a quality remindful more of Stratford or London than of Tokyo. "I should have paid more attention to time than to you. Again."

But all she did was show him a wider smile. He turned to Tony. "I apologize for having to ask you, but—are you going with the crew this morning?—will you be able to take us to the location?"

"Yes. That's one of the reasons I'm hanging around here this morning—rounding up strays. Let's go."

Tony spread his arms and sort of shooed them across the lot to the Bronco.

"You're sure this is no trouble?" Dennis asked.

"No trouble," Tony said.

After they settled in—Tony at the wheel, Dennis in the front seat on the passenger side, Donna in the back behind Dennis—Tony went on, "Today's location is on the way to Win Miller's place; I'm going to see Win this morning; so I'll be driving by the shoot, anyway." And he swung the Bronco around and down the Reservation Road on the trail of the crew bus.

During the next few minutes he made a couple of stabs at getting a conversation started, but casual early morning chatter apparently didn't appeal to anyone else. There seemed to be a touch of testiness in the air, in addition to the lingering trace of wood smoke, so he let the road sounds take over. Dennis appeared to be absorbed in the view out the passenger side. And Donna, as Tony saw in occasional glances in the rearview mirror, gave the impression that her idea of happiness was to stare dreamily at the back of the actor's head with a soft smile on her face.

Finally, though, the interpreter had to say something to the actor; or, possibly, lover had to contact lover. She leaned forward, toward Shimada's back. And although she spoke in Japanese, there was no mistaking the warm, intimate tone in her voice. Just as, looking in the mirror, Tony couldn't mistake the look in her eyes.

So Shimada's rough reaction hit hard. Fast and cold, he snapped over his shoulder. "When I'm in Japan, I speak Japanese. When I'm in France, I speak French. This is America. Speak English. And no. The smell of wood smoke does not remind me of Japan."

Undaunted, Donna reached forward with her right hand and touched his shoulder with her fingertips. Quietly, but in English, she said, "It brings back memories of that small country inn where we—"

Shimada jerked away from her touch and her hand flopped against the car seat. "Enough."

His rejection and that single word made her rock back, her eyes closed, and despite the wind whipping through Tony's partially opened window, a sudden breathless tension filled the car.

It lasted for at least two minutes, until Shimada shifted in his seat, coughed, turned for a quick look at Tony before he said, looking straight ahead, "There is something I would like for you to do for me, Tony, please."

"Sure."

"This is completely off of the previous subject."

"Good."

"I realize that we've just a short time remaining here, but I would like to change my hotel room."

"Change your—?" Tony gave his head a sharp shake, as if he'd heard wrong. "You've been in that room for about three weeks—the picture's almost finished and you'll be going home before much longer. What's wrong with the room, all of a sudden?"

"I've asked Nobu, a couple of times. But he's always so busy he keeps forgetting."

"What's—"

"I've asked the manager but he says all the rooms are taken."

"What's wrong with—" Tony glanced in the mirror at Donna but she was staring out her window, her face blank.

"Nothing is wrong with the room except"—he looked quickly toward Tony and away before he rushed out with—"except that it has a shower instead of a tub and—"

"A *tub*?"

"—and I prefer a tub for bathing."

"A tub?"

"*Any* Japanese, in fact, prefers a tub bath." In the mirror, Tony saw Donna, still looking out the window, nodding slowly in agreement. "I have kept the room without major objections because I didn't want to make additional problems for Nobu. Or for you. I know you both have many other things to do." Shimada paused. "I also know that this may sound strange to you. Possibly trivial. But I sincerely want a change."

Tony shrugged. "That's easy. Just switch rooms with me. That shouldn't cause anybody a problem."

FIVE

Wednesday (continued)

THE REST OF the drive continued in silence, and when they arrived at the location and the actor and the interpreter got out, still the only sounds Tony heard were the Bronco doors opening and slamming shut.

Musing on the wondrous ways of semi-true love on a sunny summer morning, he drove on along the little county road and turned south onto Highway 97 toward the Miller place. And when he turned up the bumpy, rocky dirt approach to the house, set on a slight rise, he was surprised—again—by the wild-animal screams of the two huge peacocks that suddenly swooped in over the hood of the Bronco and landed a few feet in front of it.

They spread their spotted blue-green wings and stalked ahead of him in their teetering longlegged gait, fluorescent tail feathers dragging through the dust, leading him slowly up the trail with a series of raucous, screeching screams that rousted a flock of starlings out of the willow grove surrounding the Miller's Carpenter Gothic farmhouse, set a dog yapping behind one of the lace-curtained bay windows, and brought seven or eight Rhode Island Reds swirling, flapping and squawking out through a hole in a rusty wire chicken coop slumped against the left end of a long, narrow, doorless cinder-block shed that faced the house across the driveway and served as garage, storage area, and bird sanctuary.

The peacock screeches also made Gramp Miller look toward the house from the gambrel-roofed barn a hundred yards away.

Waving at Gramp as the old man started toward him, Tony climbed down from the Bronco, shaking his head in admiration of Miller's vigorous walk. "Seventy-plus, and look at him go."

The churning way he walked reminded Tony of one of those limited-animation cartoon characters whose arms and legs move in a blur while the torso stays still. That's the way Gramp Miller moved—upper body rigid as a post, arms swinging stiff from the shoulders, short quick steps, knees never straight, feet skimming over the ground.

Waiting for Miller to cross the barnyard Tony turned and studied the shed. Its top row of cinder blocks, sheltered under the overhanging roof at one end, showed that someone had once laid on a coat of dark green paint. But time, dust, wind, and the Central Oregon sun had faded the rest of the shed to a thin, yellowish lime.

The roof itself, rusty and wrinkled corrugated steel, looked as though its left end had come loose and started slipping off the back side but had somehow puckered up and grabbed the cornerpost at the last minute.

In the open side of the sixty-foot-long shed, four-by-four posts planted ten feet apart indicated that there'd once been a plan to divide the interior into a series of bays, probably with doors, for parking trucks, tractors, and other farm equipment out of the weather. But that plan must've been abandoned long ago. The dirt floor, what could be seen of it, had been taken over by crabgrass, dandelions, and a large crop of thistles, some standing three to four feet tall.

Inside the shed but exposed to the weather and other elements by the missing section of roof, an old and once-red Chevy Luv pickup truck stood sadly on flat, lopsided tires.

Tony knew that the truck had originally been red because he saw traces of pink peeking up through layers, mounds, hillocks, and globs of guano deposited over it by generation upon generation of chickens, blackbirds, barn swallows, starlings, owls, pigeons, meadowlarks, blue jays, magpies, and peacocks. By donating droppings over the windshield, body, cab, and bed of the truck they'd created an off-white semigloss that Chevrolet never dreamed of.

The truck bed was now a handy bin for storing empty beer bottles and cans and six-packs, soft drink cans, bourbon bottles, paint buckets, rolls of rusty chicken wire, and scraps of wood and plasterboard.

A tall metal stepladder leaned against the truck's passenger door, a shorter one against the right front fender. Five scarred old wooden sawhorses stood stacked astraddle each other in the middle of a ring of cut and punctured truck and tractor tires. Two ancient metal tool chests stood open and empty against the back wall. Lining the wall was a row of useless old wood doors, some standing upright, others on their sides, their windows punched out and dark bare rectangles showing where three bent and useless center pivots from irrigation systems were dumped over a scattering of four-inch pipe elbows and T's, fishing poles and dip nets, and rusty oil and gasoline cans.

At the far end of the shed, outside, a green John Deere tractor stood behind two fifty-gallon oil drums that looked as though the only thing holding them upright was rust. One was stuffed with tight tangled rolls of chicken wire. The other had a smelly, smoldering fire inside it, with a thread of blue smoke drifting upward in a lazy series of Z's and S's.

The chickens and peacocks were quiet now, but the dog still barked behind the side window of the house and as Gramp Miller came into view the barking seemed to get more frenzied.

Tony turned away from the shed and looked through the window. A chair, probably one of those naugahyde recliners, had been drawn up with its back close to the glass. Lace curtains draped like a frame around the chair and the little straggly-haired Cairn terrier teetered on its slick, narrow top.

The dog barked again, lost his balance and flipped out of sight, skidding backwards onto the chair seat. Clawing frantically, he scrambled up, growling a high-pitched growl as though talking to himself. Once more, balanced on his toenails, he barked and disappeared again. He clawed his way back up, front toenails first, then wet black nose, oversized hairy head, quivering little shoulders and rear end.

"Ain't that pitiful?" Gramp Miller, standing beside Tony, ducked his blocky white head toward the yapping, scrambling dog. "If that sorry little sumbitch was a fish you'd throw him back." Tony grinned down at him, into clear, innocent blue eyes that seemed both amused and sad when he looked up at Tony and back at the dog and back at Tony again. "You're the fella from the *tee*-vee, right?"

"That's right, Mr. Miller. Tony Pratt." He held out his hand and Miller gripped it. His hand was like the rest of him, stubby and strong.

"I thought I said to call me 'Gramp' like everybody else."

Tony still couldn't believe that Miller was in his seventies. "Yes, sir."

Rugged and active, Gramp Miller was about five-and-a-half feet tall, his body wide and thick in hickory-type overalls. Strong, stubby arms sunburned the color of roofing tile poked out of his faded blue short-sleeve work shirt. "And you can forget the 'sir,' too."

Tony waved a hand toward the window. "Is that the family dog?"

"Pet. That's not a dog. That's a pet. A dog you can let outside without wonderin' if the squirrels're gonna carry him home for supper."

Miller shook his head, staring at the dog. "No, that's Jo's pet. 'A present,' she said." He turned his back to the dog. "But if somebody give *me* a thing like that, my own personal opinion is it'd be some kind of a joke. But Jo's happy, so..."

He started walking away, leading Tony toward the tractor at the end of the shed. "Come on. If we get out of sight maybe he'll shut up." He glanced back over his shoulder at the frenetic little dog. "Every time he starts doin' that I keep hopin' the damn fool thing'll have a heart attack, but no such luck. What's on your mind?"

"Just want to make sure we're all set for that 'roundup' we plan to stage with some of your cattle."

"Right. We're all set. Even lined up a few extra riders—couple o' neighbor kids in case you need help with the animals."

"Good, they may come in handy. And I wanted to tell you that we've changed our schedule since the last time I talked with you. Now we'd like to shoot a little sooner than we talked about."

"Okay with me. Fact is, Win and Jo and JayDee're out right now with the cattle you're gonna use, bringin' 'em to a closer piece of ground. That way it won't take so long to get 'em when you're ready."

"Fine. How's Friday. Is that too soon for you?"

"No, that's okay. Don't make me no never mind." Gramp shrugged and gave a little laugh. "Might fuddle the cattle a mite, though."

"How's that?"

"Gettin' their pictures took by a bunch of Japs on horseback."

There was a silence. Tony looked away toward the barn and the distant hills, then back at Gramp and away again.

"Somethin' botherin' you?"

Tony took a deep breath and looked down at the bright blue eyes, now narrowed, squinting back at him. "I'm sorry, Mr. Miller—"

"'Gramp,' I said."

"—but I think people should be given a chance and—"

"No need to be sorry about somethin' you believe."

"—and I don't believe in calling people names like 'Japs.'"

"*You* can call 'em whatever you want but the Japs killed my kid brother at Pearl Harbor."

"I'm sorry—"

"I can still feel it, this very second—"

"—but that was a long time ago."

"—the hurt I felt when Daddy told me, standin' right over there on the back porch o' that very same house. And that very same day—married or not, kids or not—I went in and signed up. I walked into Conroy—nobody'd carry me over there, so I walked into Conroy, caught a bus to Portland and I signed up and spent four years in the Pacific killin' the people that killed my brother."

"But these people had nothing to do with that—they weren't even *born* when—"

Gramp raised his left hand in a stopping gesture. His hand had been spread flat on the fender of the tractor, pressing so hard the skin was white around his fingernails and when he raised that hand Tony half-expected to see dents in the fender.

"Let me finish," Gramp said. "You told me about you, I'm tellin' you about me. And a few others around here." He ducked his head, looking out past the barn. Walking slowly toward it on the faint trail that disappeared over a rise about a half-mile away, two riders were leading a third horse. A pickup truck rolled along beside the riders.

Leaning into the tractor, Gramp went on. His words came out fast and bitter. "So we won the war and I come home but I'll be damned if we're not in *another* one not much later. Korea. So off goes my son Win to get *his* butt shot at. And after he comes outta *that* with just a couple o' teeny holes in him, I'll be go-to-hell if there ain't *another* war out there in the Pacific and away goes *his* kid. Vietnam! for chrissakes, wherever the hell that is. And Win's boy—my grandson''—he slapped his hands together with a crack—''dead.'' He jammed his hands in his back pockets so hard he leaned backwards. ''And he's still there somewhere.''

He looked at Tony and his eyes were cold and hard behind the tears. ''So I got no love for these people you're workin' with—Japs, Koreans, South Vietnams, whatever. There's only one reason we're doin' this, and that's because people from the state and the county and the town say it'll help bring in tourist business and money.''

Gramp rubbed the back of his hand across his eyes and then scrubbed roughly at his short-cut gray hair. ''Sounds kinda far-fetched to me, but that's what they say so we'll go along with it and we'll help you get your job done.''

He turned away to watch his son, his granddaughter, and the hired hand as they got closer to the barn. ''I thought it best for you to know that, if it wasn't for that aspect of it, if one of those people you're workin' with was to step foot on this land he just might get his ass shot off.'' He nodded toward the people approaching. ''And except for Jo, there, ever'body you see right now feels the same way.''

WHEN HE MADE his usual call to Pat from his room that night, Tony gave her a full description of the emotional scenes he'd been through during the day.

Her response included a little worry mixed with a touch of laughter. "Sounds as though your quiet little Japanese family TV show is turning into a made-in-Hollywood melodrama."

"Does sound a little soapy, doesn't it?"

"Just make sure you don't get caught in the middle when all those passions begin to burn."

"Jack-be-nimble, huh?"

"Something like that. But speaking of passion—"

"Ah ha."

"—my work is all caught up so I'm yours for a long weekend."

"That'll be nice. Very, very nice."

SIX

Thursday

THE NEXT MORNING at ten Pat left a "take care of the place, see you Sunday" note on the kitchen counter for Jenny and Dan, wondering—again—at the ability of kids home from college to work seven hours and sleep twelve.

In the garage she set her small suitcase and her overnight case on the back seat of the Volvo wagon, opened and closed the garage door quietly, and just as quietly drove away from their house in the small Portland suburb of Lakewood. Crossing the Willamette River on the I-205 bridge, Pat caught a glimpse of Mt. Hood rising tall and white-topped against the bright blue sky. The sky itself was clear and cloudless except for a little smudge of smoke on the other side of the mountain.

She headed for State Highway 212 and rode it east through the town with one of her two favorite names in the state—Boring. Her other favorite in this rainy part of the world was a town named Drain.

She left 212 for Highway 26, climbing the west flank of Mt. Hood past some other nice names—Zig Zag,

Rhododendron. Then the road, carved out of the mountainside, turned seriously up.

On her right the steep fir-covered slope dropped away into deep green ravines, but flattened a bit every now and then to hold a small meadow speckled with buttercups, or a sky-blue lake glistening in the sun.

Across the ravines, great green trees marched up the other side and spread for seemingly endless miles, scarred here and there by bald, clear-cut squares or the thin stripe of a fire trail.

In the distance, stretching in a long, ragged line toward California, Mt. Jefferson and other snow-capped peaks of the Cascade Range stood like echoes of Mt. Hood—Mt. Bachelor, The Sisters, Broken Top, Three-Finger Jack, and the others that gave Nine Mountain Lake its name.

Driving on past Government Camp and the turnoff to Timberline Lodge—which, at six-thousand feet, was slightly more than half-way up Mt. Hood—Pat felt the road begin descending and changing direction, curving around from almost due east to south and east.

After a few more miles she drove by a big rectangular sign: "Entering The Short Falls Indian Reservation." The sign made her realize, with a happy sense of surprise, that she was more than midway through her three-hour drive. She rolled the window down, feeling the snow-and-glacier-touched temperature changing from cold to cool on its way to high-desert warm—smelling the vegetation beginning to vary from Douglas firs and cedars to sagebrush and ponderosa pine.

But despite the loveliness of the day—bright sunshine, deep blue sky, cloudless except for that smoke, which she'd seen before as a smudge and was now a tall blue-white column rising from some kind of fire far ahead on her right—despite the lovely day, Pat couldn't help but be aware that she was driving down the side of a volcano. The violent and deadly eruption of Mt. St. Helens was not so long ago or far away that she'd forgotten about it—May 18, 1980 to be precise, and only fifty miles north in Washington State.

She was, in fact, recalling bits and pieces from the worn copy of a book called *Roadside Geology* that she and Tony kept in the car.

"Mt. Hood—Oregon's most spectacular volcano—"

"Think of it as just another mountain," she told herself.

"—great height and steep profile typical—hasn't erupted for probably thousands of years—"

"Good."

"—one of its last acts was to squeeze up a nearly solid plug of magma—this often signals end of volcanic activity—but can't be sure about that."

"Hmm," she said to herself.

"If Mt. Hood should erupt..."

"Well, enough of that."

The highway was stepping down now—a flat stretch, then descending, another flat stretch, then another shallow descent—and the stands of trees were sparser. She could see the reddish, plate-like bark of ponderosas among the darker trunks of firs, and Scotch broom along the roadside. Far off she could see an occasional tall, conical, reddish-brown hill standing abruptly in a flat, sagebrush plain.

"Cinder cones," she said.

"...start erupting off in a field somewhere, cough chunks of magma out of their vent...build a cone of cinders a few hundred feet high...one or two lava flows from base...once they quit, never erupt again."

"Good. Happy to hear it," Pat said.

The cinder cones were interspersed with low, wide mounds that rose and fell across the lane like ocean swells.

"...shield volcanoes...broad domes formed of repeated basalt eruptions from same vent...broad and flat because basalt is such fluid magma...never very conspicuous... Cascades full of big ones that people never notice."

"And lava caves. I've love to see a lava cave."

"...form when outer surface of lava flow cools and solidifies...inside still molten...fluid magma within runs out from under solid crust, leaving hollow inside..."

Looking ahead several miles, Pat could see more of the Cascade Range and rolling hills and great flat-topped buttes that seemed supported by thick columns of rock.

"—*columnar basalt*—"

"All right! Enough. Change the subject."

In the near distance, the road ran comparatively flat and straight ahead.

There was the bridge across the canyon of the Short Falls River, then came the town of Madras, and then the rolling plateau that holds Barlow County and Conroy.

But she wouldn't have to cross the bridge; Tony would be at the Reservation Lodge and he'd reminded her that the turnoff to the reservation was about a half-mile west of the bridge. "It'll be on your right," he'd said. "If you get to the bridge, you've gone too far."

Pat frowned. "On the right." She said it aloud, worry in her voice. "Where that smoke is?" The base of the column of smoke had grown wider and turned black, as it boiled upward the black and grey and blue-white smoke mixed together and made a long, ugly scar in the bright blue sky.

A siren screamed in Pat's left ear and snapped her back from her near reverie. A pickup truck roared by. At least ten men stood or crouched in the bed holding axes and shovels.

Instinctively she slowed a little, suddenly aware that she didn't have this two-lane highway to herself anymore. Out of nowhere, through wide empty fields on side roads she'd never seen or even suspected, came pickups and stake-bed trucks with more men and boys. Trailing rooster-tails of dust, the truck bounced and skidded onto the highway, boys and men grabbing and clutching anything they could to stay in the truck.

Flashing red-and-white lights appeared suddenly in her rearview mirror. Pat glanced up and saw another truck coming up. She looked at the road and when she looked back at the mirror she saw nothing but the grinning teeth of the truck's metal grill, so close that it could have been in the back seat.

With a roar the grill disappeared and the truck came swerving around and she glimpsed a sheriff's insignia on the side door as the truck screamed past.

Pat slowed a little more. Down the road the trucks and cars made a right-angle turn off the main road and began to climb the ridge to her right. At the same time, coming from the east in the other lane, four sets of flashing red lights showed more emergency vehicles on the way.

She passed a big, weathered sign reading, "Reservation Lodge, Short Falls Indian Reservation, Exit 500 ft."

Halfway to the exit, Pat flipped her right-turn signal. Just then, a big white car appeared in her side mirror with red-and-blue lights whirling on top and she recognized an Oregon State Police car before it zoomed past.

At the reservation turnoff, the state car rocked off the highway onto the shoulder and, churning up a cloud of dust, made a U-turn back onto the highway and stopped in the center, all lights whirling and flashing to warn oncoming cars.

The officer hopped out, pulling on his Smokey Bear hat and walking up the road toward Pat, waving her off to the side.

She pulled over and stopped. The officer turned to go back to the intersection. Pat jumped out to run after him and a blast of wind almost knocked her down.

In the car, she hadn't noticed any wind at all. Now it plastered her tan seersucker dress against her legs and breasts, pulled at her salt-and-pepper hair. She yanked her neck scarf off and retied it around her head, squinting against the wind and blowing dirt. Dust devils spun down the shoulder of the road. On the other side of the drainage ditch, the three rusty strands of an old barbed wire fence swung back and forth. Behind the fence, a few tall ponderosas swayed gracefully, sailing dead brown needles through the air. In the fields, sagebrush shook with the wind and mullein stalks dipped and waved yellow flowers.

The Oregon State Police officer looked back at her from thirty feet away but continued waking. Realizing who he was, Pat shouted. "Officer Kelsey!"

He looked back again and stopped. By this time the emergency vehicles coming from the east were roaring into the turn up Reservation Road toward The Lodge. Five or six cars waited at the intersection while they passed, and more cars were coming down.

When Kelsey nodded and spoke, Pat saw rather than heard, "Well, hello Mrs. Pratt."

In rapid succession, four pickup trucks skidded squealing onto the curving access road. The first three were painted a faded, peeling red. Each had a hose reel and water tank mounted in the back, and "Volunteer Fire Department" painted on the door, one from Madras, one from Conroy, and the third from Terrebonne, a little town south of Conroy. The fourth truck was green, with the Short Falls Indian Reservation logo on its door and a load of Indian men and boys in back, crouching, kneeling, and looking tense and worried.

Hurrying on toward Officer Kelsey, Pat felt as though she were screaming over the truck noise. "What's going on? I have to get to The Lodge."

Kelsey's eyes were hidden behind his sunglasses, but she saw his frown and the grim look of his mouth. "Sorry, Mrs. Pratt. Emergency vehicles only up there now."

"What's the smoke—forest fire?"

"Yes, ma'am. And there's one report that it's got The Lodge."

Pat's knees went weak and she fell back a step, looking toward the thick black smoke. Without seeing it, she watched a dented and dirty yellow pickup climbing Reservation Road with one brake light flashing when it slowed for a curve.

Her voice sounded like a scream when Pat grabbed at Kelsey's arms. "But Tony's up there!"

TONY AND NOBU had talked it over with The Lodge's manager the night before.

Everybody at The Lodge knew that a slash fire had burst out of control and jumped into a thick stand of ponderosa pine. Everybody knew that it was burning into the shallow valley about a mile to the west, behind the wide range that held The Lodge perched on its east slope. But nobody knew where the fire would burn next or if The Lodge was in danger.

What wind there was was out of the south. If it shifted to the west, it could easily drive the fire across the valley and up the ridge. Once over the ridge crest, the fire would swiftly sweep through the long, dry prairie grass and down on The Lodge.

The manager—William Edmonds, also a member of the Short Falls Tribal Council—felt that The Lodge and its three hundred guests were in no danger.

"I'm not planning to evacuate the guests *or* the staff," he'd said, "because I know that the Reservation Fire Department can handle the situation, with help from the Forest Service, if necessary." His recommendation to Nobu was "business as usual—you and your crew go ahead with your work and stick to your schedule."

Nobu and Tony accepted the manager's analysis and agreed to go on shooting. However, between themselves they agreed on something else.

So this morning, as usual, Nobu and most of the crew took off for the day's location. But four of the crew stayed at The Lodge with Tony, to gather equipment and personal gear and move it out if the evacuation order came.

It was a hectic, nerve-racking morning. Nobody had slept well. All night long, beyond the ridge, thick clouds of smoke boiled up, glowing with shades of red reflected from the fires below. The smoke was so thick and its strength so strong that the hotel's air-conditioning system was virtually useless.

Just before seven o'clock the air got even dirtier when reservation firemen jockeyed a bulldozer along the crest of the ridge, churning up great clouds of billowing red dust as they tried to cut a firebreak through the long, dry prairie grass.

Fire trucks chugged up Reservation Road from as far east as Bend and as far west as Sandy and Gresham. Volunteer firemen came to help from little towns and villages all over Central Oregon. They drove around behind The Lodge and a few parked their trucks to form a protective arc up-slope from the hotel's rear deck. Most of the men hurried on down a narrow trail around the ridge, toward the smoke rising from the valley behind it.

By nine o'clock the fire fighters sent word that they'd cut the fire off to the north, west, and south; the only remaining "hot spot," as they called it, was on the backside of the ridge above The Lodge; they were sure that the firebreak would contain it and it would soon burn itself out.

But fear of the fire had already affected the hotel guests, especially those with small children. Their fear, aggravated by the smoky, dirty, irritating air and by the nearly constant parade of rattling, creaking equipment, made more than half of the guests pack up and leave.

At ten o'clock, standing with the four Japanese crewmen, Tony watched another noisy, nervous, red-eyed family haul their luggage through the lobby. The mother, in the manner of all mothers, kept track of the father while she counted suitcases and toys, checked for clean faces and hands, and talked to the children.

"Are you sure they weren't squirrels?" she asked.

"Yes," the ten-year-old girl said. "They were chipmunks. I saw squirrels, too, but these were chipmunks."

"And a couple of rabbits," said her eight-year-old brother, "running away from the fire, I guess. And snakes."

"What?" He got the mother's full attention.

"Snakes."

"Where? Where!" Her head swiveled around.

"Outside," he said. "Slithering through the grass."

"Toward the hotel," his sister said.

"Prob'ly garter snakes," said the boy. "But maybe rattlers."

"Ich," said his mother, shivering. "I'm glad we're getting out of here."

Through the big front window Tony watched them toss their stuff into their car, the mother keeping a constant lookout for snakes. As they drove away, he suddenly remembered that Pat had planned to leave Lakewood about this time and drive over to join him.

He tried to call her on one of the lobby phones, to tell her not to come to The Lodge, to meet him in Conroy. No answer. No Pat, no kids.

At that moment a roar crashed over The Lodge. People started rushing across the lobby toward the rear door and out to the deck on the hotel's uphill side. Tony hurried out with the crowd in time to see a huge silver tanker plane drop its liquid load toward a line of flames flicking through the parched brown grass on the crest of the ridge. A blast of wind blew over the crest. It hit the falling liquid ball, spreading it into a thin curtain that swung through the air, transparent, in front of the boiling black column of smoke. Then the curtain split, ripped apart, and disintegrated into a lacy, ineffectual spray blowing downhill away from the flames and toward The Lodge.

Standing on the back deck, Tony felt a few drops of liquid on his face. The wind had shifted.

He focused on the top of the slope. Black ashes, embers, and flaming twigs flew through the air, blown up from the other side and over the crest. Sailing on the wind they crossed the firebreak and fell into the grass where wisps of gray-blue smoke stretched in a thin, waving line for almost a hundred yards along the side of the slope.

Another gust blew down the slope before Tony heard a loud whooshing sound. The smoke disappeared for a split second before flames flashed along that same hundred yards and the fire exploded through the grass toward The Lodge.

From that point, as Tony told Pat later, the fire fighting was "focused chaos. Not organized, Lord knows, but focused on beating the fire."

The bulldozer driver tried cutting another break in front of the fire to turn it back on itself but its engine died halfway across the crest. That slowed the fire a little but then the fire trucks with water tanks ran out of water. Then the pump bringing water from the Short Falls River broke down.

By this time the flames had licked and blown across the break. Edmonds, the manager, raced through the hotel asking for help. All the men who could move, and some women, joined up as volunteer fire fighters. Hotel staff, hotel guests, Tony, the four Japanese TV crew—all worked frantically through the morning and afternoon on the fire line, some with spades and shovels, some in a bucket brigade hauling water from the swimming pool, some soaking blankets and burlap bags in the pool and spreading them over the grass.

Finally, around six-thirty, the fire was out. Tony straightened, stretching his back. He stuck his spade in the ground and looked around, leaning on the warm wood handle. The hillside was burned black except for a narrow strip of dry grass along the back of The Lodge. Another ten yards and the fire would have got it. He felt like letting out a cheer—for himself and for the thin line of tired, sweaty, soot-blackened volunteers that had just beaten a wildfire, almost with their bare hands. What stopped him was the startling sight of JayDee Hampton leaning on a shovel and looking back at him from the other end of the line.

And just then he heard the pump start working to bring up water from the river.

SEVEN

Thursday (continued)

BY SUNSET it was over and manager William Edmonds invited them all to a celebration. His dining room staff stripped off the starched white tablecloths—no fool, Edmonds saw how dirty everybody was—shoved some tables together for a buffet, and laid out beer, soft drinks, iced tea, beef, ham, and turkey. Then he and his guests and/or fire fighters—professional, volunteer, and amateur—celebrated saving The Lodge.

And everybody who didn't have to get back to their firehouse, farm, business, or home piled in. Most of them hadn't eaten since breakfast.

Grabbing a beer, Tony plowed back through the crowd and up the three steps between the dining room and lobby. Half-sitting, half-leaning on the wood railing separating the two, he looked out over the crowd and sipped his beer as he wondered how to get in touch with Pat.

One of the volunteer firemen stopped beside him, the neck of an ice-cold beer bottle in each hand. Waving one of his bottles around at the crowd he said to Tony, "Everybody in this place is dirty as a mud road and smelly as a goat. But I'm proud to be here with 'em."

"Ain't we all," Tony said. "Dirty and proud."

The fireman's brown work boots, blue jeans, and red T-shirt were almost black with rubbed-in ashes and dirt. Below his bloodshot eyes, sweat and smoky tears running down his face had left ragged pale trails through the dirt and beard stubble on his cheeks and jaws. Even his ears and neck looked sooty. The only place his face looked clean was the clear strip across his forehead where his dirty red baseball cap had sat.

Now the cap sat back on his head a little, but Tony could still read the patch sewn on the front of the crown. It was the outline of a big valentine's heart; inside the heart was the rear end of a jackass; outside, it said, "My heart is in farming but my ass is in debt."

Tony grinned a tired grin, saluting the fireman with his bottle of beer.

The fireman raised the bottle of beer in his left hand and drank it straight down without stopping. Then he raised his right-hand bottle and drank it straight down. When he finished, he spread his arms wide toward the crowd in the dining-room, turned both bottles upside down, and belched a belch that rang the glass chandelier. There was immediate silence. Followed by a roar of approval and a round of applause. Followed by Pat's voice in Tony's ear saying, "So this is your idea of a quiet weekend, huh?"

Tony spun around. He caught a glimpse of Sergeant Kelsey behind her before he wrapped his arms around Pat's waist and she threw her arms around his neck and she was saying, "Are you all right, are you okay?" and "You smell like a barbecue" and "What are you trying to do, make the nice lady's hair turn gray?"

After that, Tony found a table where they could all sit, eat, and drink while he told them about the fire. Then Kelsey finished his coffee and left just as the television crew came back, so Tony introduced Pat to Nobu and some of the Japanese staff and began repeating his story of the fire while the celebration swirled all around.

With all of this going on, nobody paid any attention to the figure that slipped in from the back deck and turned left, hurrying along the far wall of the lobby toward the stairs. He carried a lumpy burlap bag in his left hand, shielding it with his body as much as possible to keep it out of sight. His gloved fist held the bag shut like a drawstring and his arm stretched far away from his body. It was an awkward way to carry the big bag but he got inside and up the stairs fast.

On the second floor he hurried down the hallway turning his head from side to side, checking room numbers. At Room 234 he stopped and opened the door with a key.

Quickly but carefully he swung the gunny sack ahead of him as he stepped through the opening then reached back to almost-close the door behind him. Without turning on a light he stepped farther into the room, cautiously, then looked back quickly, judging the distance to the narrow strip of light beside the open door. He took two more steps and stopped at the foot of the bed to look around the room.

Sliding glass doors in front let in enough light to see a table and two chairs silhouetted in front of the doors, the bed on the right, dresser on the left, telephone on the dresser.

He went to the dresser and stooped, taking care not to bump the bag against the dresser or the floor. Reaching down with his free hand he moved the wastebasket sitting beside the dresser and in front of the telephone jack in the wall. Then he grabbed the telephone line and jerked it out of the wall. When he dropped the frayed end of the cord it hit the metal wastebasket with a little tinging sound.

He straightened and stepped back one step, glancing over his shoulder again toward the door. He paused for a long, deep breath and flexed his knees. Then he grabbed a bottom corner of the bag with his left hand, letting go of the top with his right to grab the other corner. He flipped the bag upside down and dumped the contents into the room as he scuttled rapidly backward toward the door. Without opening the door any wider he tried to back through the narrow space but he bumped the door frame and something snagged the back of his belt. "Shit!" As soon as he said it a whirring rattle came from inside the room.

He jerked free and something fell on his boot and bounced behind him onto the hall carpet. He pulled the door closed with a click that seemed to set off another quicker, louder rattle that came through the door as he ran down the hall.

He stopped at the stairway, pulled off his gloves, folded them together, and jammed them in a hip pocket. Then he walked casually down the stairs and into the noisy celebration where somebody with a guitar was leading the crowd in singing, of all things, "On Top of Old Smokey."

He moved left along the edge of the crowd toward the reception desk, picking up an abandoned bottle of beer on the way. When he got to the reception desk he started to cross the lobby but appeared to be blocked by the crowd. He stopped, shrugged helplessly, then noticed the empty aisle behind the desk where the clerks and cashier usually work. Now, with the celebration going on and no one behind the counter, it offered the only unobstructed path across the lobby.

He stepped around the pillar at the end and walked along slowly, behind the desk. He was looking out at the crowded lobby, to his right, when he came to the rack for room keys, on his left. Suddenly, with his right hand, he waved the beer bottle at someone in the crowd while his left hand slid a key into slot 234 and, without stopping or breaking step, he walked on to the other end of the reception desk.

He paused long enough to drop the empty bottle into a wastebasket and to glance back to make sure he'd got the key in the right slot. Then he swung around the reception desk and disappeared among the other dirty jeans, dirty shirts, and dirty straw Stetsons just as Tony and Pat came through the front door with Pat's luggage.

After saying goodnight to Nobu and the others they'd gone out to get Pat's things and lock the car for the night. They'd had enough celebration, enough food and drink, enough talk of the fire, and now they were eager to get into their room, their shower, and their bed.

Tony eased them through the crush to the reception desk. Seeing nobody behind it, he wagged his head for Pat to follow him down the empty aisle past the key rack, where he plucked the key from slot 336.

They were waiting at the elevator when he said, "Whoa. I forgot."

"What?"

"I traded rooms with Shimada." And they went back to replace his old key and pick up the key to 234.

"It's just one flight," he said. "Let's walk."

As they started up the stairs Pat noticed a burlap bag draped over the newel post. "Something left over from fighting the fire?"

He shrugged a shoulder. "Maybe somebody's planning to take home the leftover beer."

When they got to the second floor Pat stopped and put her head on his shoulder for a second. Tony bent his head over and brushed his cheek against her hair. "Tired?"

She nodded, straightening. "Bet you are, too."

They started down the hall. "Yes. Looking forward to a hot shower, though."

"Not I. For a change I'm going to have a good, long tub-soak."

He stopped and moaned a low, "Oh, no."

"Now what?"

"There's no tub in here," he said, pointing the key at the door. "That's why I traded with Shimada—so he could have a tub." He put the key in the lock. "I'm sorry. You'll have to settle for a shower."

"In that case, you'll have to scrub my back."

"Gladly." He opened the door, ushering her in. "And any other service that madam may require..." Following Pat into the room Tony shoved the door with his elbow, flipping the light switch as he passed it, but he stopped in his tracks when Pat let out a startled gasp and a loud rattling buzz filled the room. "*Jee*-zus!"

Pat stood petrified in front of the bed, pointing. Between her and the sliding glass door a rattlesnake curled and coiled into its defensive posture.

Before Tony could say anything more, a movement made him look down to his left as another snake slithered toward the hallway. But the swinging door slammed shut and the second rattler curled and coiled in front of it.

"Don't move!" he told Pat, shouting, because the buzzing rattle sounded loud enough to be heard down the hall and all the way downstairs and because the snakes looked as big as fire hoses.

"Tony, what're we going to do?" Her voice was thin, shaking.

And when Tony answered his came out high and reedy, as if someone had a grip on his throat. "I don't know. Stay still."

They stood. The snake noise faded some.

"Can we call for help?"

He saw the phone, almost within reach on the dresser. "Yes." Then he saw the frayed end of the cord on the floor by the wastebasket. "No."

"What?"

"It's pulled out of the wall."

"What?"

"It doesn't work!" He took a breath to calm himself a little. "Stay quiet." He looked around. The rattles stopped but the snakes stayed poised, heads high and moving back and forth slowly, sensors searching for motion.

He was at the foot of the bed, facing the left wall. Pat was on his right, two feet away, between bed and dresser. Dresser on her left, against the left wall. Left of the dresser, a foot of blank wall, then a corner. Around the corner a short hallway, maybe two steps long, led to the bathroom. The door was open. Left of the bathroom door in that hallway, the closet door. Closed. Left of the closet and around another corner, a little recess about three feet deep. The hall door, the only way out, was on the back wall of that recess. And the rattlesnake was in front of the door.

He looked back to Pat. There was a rattle but he tried to ignore it. "Honey, turn your head. Just your head! No, the other way."

"Okay. But what're we doing?"

"See the bathroom?"

"No. The corner is in the way."

"Okay. Look past the corner. See the closet?"

"I see the door, yes."

"It's in a little hallway—about a two-step hall-way—and the john is next to it."

"So?"

"And the john door is open."

"So?"

"So listen: What I'll do is, I'm gonna toss your duffle at the hall door. Away from the snake. Maybe that'll get his attention, get him looking in the other direction, maybe. So you can get into that john."

"What do you mean, 'maybe'?" Before he could answer, she went on, "But what about you, what'll *you* do?"

"Stand still!" He took another deep breath. "I'll think of something."

"But—"

"Please don't 'but' me, Pat. I just want to get you behind that door."

They were both suddenly quiet, watching the snakes, frightened and almost hypnotized by the flat, wedge-shaped heads weaving and watching back with cold, bulging eyes glittering, unblinking. The silence was almost more frightening than the rattles. Tony and Pat seemed to hear each other's hearts.

In her soft, still-scared voice she said, "But I thought snakebites weren't fatal unless you were out in the wild—unless you couldn't get help for a couple of hours."

Tony nodded while slowly raising the bright blue duffle bag to chest height. "I've heard that, too." Now he held the bag under his chin with both hands. "It's an idea that I don't want to test. How 'bout you?"

After a pause she shook her head once. "No."

"Right. So. I'm gonna toss this bag. Be ready to go—fast—and when you get inside the john, slam the door."

"But what about this *other* snake?"

"I think he's far enough away. I think he won't move if you're going away from him. How do *I* know! What do *I* know from snakes? All I know is what I read in the books! Don't argue and when I say go, go! And slam that door!"

The buzzing started again.

"Stop yelling at me!—you're getting them all excited!"

The buzzing rattle got loud.

"Ready!" Tony said.

"Yes."

"Here goes the bag." The duffle sailed up in an arc toward the door where, the instant Tony moved, the rattlesnake froze. The rattle got more intense and the snake's head swung toward the bag. The bag banged against the door and Tony yelled "Go!"

Pat spun around and ran. The rattlesnake's head pulled back. The bag hit the floor and the snake struck at the bag as Pat flung around the corner and ran into the john and slammed the door and screamed "Tonyyyy!"

When she ran by, Tony reached behind her and grabbed the wastebasket, glancing at the other rattler which started toward Pat as soon as she moved but then stopped, head up and swiveling fast, searching.

The snake by the door had moved away from the duffle, out of the recess, slightly into the room.

Watching the snakes—first one, then the other, but mostly the one near the hall door—Tony crouched at the side of the bed. He held the metal wastebasket upside down in his left hand. With his right, he started loosening the quilted bedspread, pulling it toward his corner of the bed.

Pat called from the bathroom, teary and worried. "Tony?"

"All right. It's all right."

"What're you doing?"

"Son-of-a-bitch if *I* know."

"What?"

Louder he said, "Get ready to come out o' there in a hurry."

"When?"

"I'll tell you."

Every time he pulled at the bedspread he folded it back on itself so that it gathered, accordionlike, under his hand. When he had the cover all stacked up, he grabbed an edge and then slid his forearm under the pile. With the cover draped over his arm, he stood up and called to Pat. "Ready?"

"For what?"

"When I yell, come out. Fast as you can."

"And *then* what?"

"Out the front door."

"But the snake's there!"

"He won't be. Let's go!"

"What about you?"

"I'll be right behind you. Ready?"

"Ready."

He took another deep breath, muttering to himself, "Let's hope this dumb idea works." He threw the bedspread out, keeping a grip on one edge, hoping for it to open in the air and fan out over the rattlesnake.

When he launched the cover, the snake stretched upwards, then coiled and jerked backwards. Only half of the spread unfolded as it flew through the air.

The snake stretched again, head rotating, then re-coiled under the cover as the open half dropped over it. The bedspread turned into a twisting, thumping mass as Tony jumped forward with the wastebasket in both hands and slammed it upside down over the lump of squirming snake under the spread. Holding the wastebasket down with both hands Tony yelled, "Now! Now!"

Still pushing down on the basket, he scuttled around it to get closer to the door.

Pat rushed out of the john and stopped, staring wide-eyed at Tony, now sitting on the wastebasket.

"Don't stop, for chrissakes, I've got a rattlesnake under my ass! Go!"

She turned and hopped over the duffle bag, slung the door open and jumped out to the hall with Tony right behind her. He stumbled on the duffle, cursed and kicked it through the doorway, lunged through after it and slammed the door. Then he fell back against it.

They grabbed each other and held on, scared, sweaty, hearts pounding.

"All right?"

Pat nodded. "You?" She felt his head move above hers and she looked up at him. "You're green. Pale and green."

"You, too."

Her arms were around his waist, his around her shoulders. She buried her head in his chest. "My hero."

"You, too."

Wrapped together, their breathing slowed, and their hearts. But then, in his arms, he felt her shoulders shaking as she cried. "Me, too," he said. He cupped one hand around the back of her head, rocking gently.

After a few moments she tilted her head and looked at him, tears sliding down her pale cheeks. But she was laughing, too.

He grunted, "Hmm?"

She sniffed. "What kind of hero says, 'I've got a rattlesnake under my ass'?"

THEY LEANED AGAINST the wall shaking and laughing and breathing deeply for a couple of minutes before starting for the stairs. Halfway there, Tony stopped, shook his head, and went back to get the duffle bag.

As he reached for it he saw a small round piece of metal beside it. "Wonder if that came off the bag somewhere when I kicked it." Muttering, he picked it up and put it in his pocket.

With their arms around each other they made it down the stairs on shaky, nearly watery legs, where

they pulled Edmonds aside and told him about the
visitors in room 234. Then Tony led Pat to the bar.

"Do you have J&B Scotch?" he asked the bar-
tender.

"Yes, sir."

"One J&B and water for my wife," he said. "And
I'll have one quadruple J&B, over ice. Easy on the
ice."

ABOUT AN hour and a half later, they were showered,
brushed, and ready for bed. And moved to a different
room.

Two men from the Reservation Fire Department
had captured the snakes and taken them away, but
Tony and Pat had no interest at all in 234. Now, one
floor up and far down the hall, they were on the small
balcony outside the sliding glass doors, taking a last
long look at the day.

Below The Lodge, a skimpy chain of lights showed
where Reservation Road ran across the hillside that
sloped down to the river canyon. The canyon and the
buttes beyond stood in moonlight shadows. Even farther away, moonlight on the snowcapped Cascades
gave the mountains a ghostlike appearance.

A car moved out of the parking area in front of The
Lodge, its headlights fanning out through the dark. As
it braked and turned onto the access road, its left taillight glowed a brighter red, but the right light flashed
white.

"Like JayDee Hampton's truck," Tony thought to himself. "Funny. Haven't seen him since the fire. Wonder what he's been doing all this time."

EIGHT

Friday

FRIDAY MORNING was a beautiful morning. The sky was cloudless, clear, sunny, blue. Here and there a few thin drifts of mist hovered over the river canyon or sifted through hillside draws dark with juniper and morning shadows. Pale gray veils reaching up for the sun's warm light, they lifted slowly till they felt its touch, then curled and twisted higher, thinning, and then disappeared like magic in the air.

The next thing that Tony and Pat noticed, on their way to breakfast in The Lodge, was no smoke—no big, thick, ugly black column of smoke shooting up into the sky just over the hill. There were no screaming sirens and no bellowing fire fighters.

When they walked into the dining room, everyone seemed quiet and unexcited. Fear of the forest fire had passed.

The memory would stay, though, as Pat said. The smell of smoke, even tired watered-down smoke, set off alarms in the brain. And that smell still wafted up from the charred forest in the valley beyond the ridge and from the burnt-black stubble spread in a dark arc on the slope behind The Lodge.

Tony and Pat arrived at the table in the center of the dining room and discovered that manager William Edmonds was on the same subject. "It'll take time to dissipate," he was saying, unbending his long body. He stood and held Pat's chair while he introduced her to Donna Hughes, the interpreter.

The manager started his day as early as the TV cast and crew, so he'd got in the habit of having breakfast most mornings with anyone in the cast who happened to be at the big round table. It accommodated ten and for a few minutes each morning it was full. Usually, though—depending on individual morning routines and work assignments each day—people were coming and going, some lingering over coffee, others eating quickly and dashing away. When Tony and Pat sat down, Edmonds and Donna were the only ones there among several dirty dishes that hadn't yet been cleared away.

"I suspect that we'll have to live with the smell of old smoke much longer than we would like." Edmonds used his quiet voice precisely and his dark brown eyes locked on the person he was talking to.

At the moment it was Donna, and her short strawberry-blonde hair shimmered as she nodded at his next comment. "But it will help us remember the lessons we've learned, so that we'll be better prepared if another disaster should strike."

The waitress came and quietly took breakfast orders from Tony and Pat while Edmonds continued.

"We're already working on a request to the Tribal Council. We want to improve the pumping system, first of all. And we want to extend the access road, continue it around the back of the building, which will also serve as a firebreak."

Abruptly he stopped. "Enough of that." Then he spoke directly to Tony and Pat. "Have you recovered from your confrontation with the snakes?"

Tony said, "Yes."

Pat said, "No."

Tony smiled quickly and said, "I guess not," before he sobered and asked Edmonds, "Have you figured out how they got in?"

"Not yet. Somebody suggested that the fire drove them inside and we were all too busy to notice." The manager shrugged. "Sounds unlikely to me. But so does the idea that the Tribal Police have. When we called them in to capture the snakes, one of the officers found a gunny sack on the stairs. He thinks the snakes may have been brought in in that."

Tony looked doubtful. "And dumped into my room?"

Pat shivered and pushed aside the eggcup that the waitress had just put down.

Edmonds shrugged again. "Who knows? But that was somebody else's room until last night, wasn't it?"

For the first time, Donna Hughes spoke. "Dennis's." Her face was paler than usual, the freckles across her cheeks more prominent.

Pat said, "D'you mean those things were meant for Dennis Shimada and we got 'em instead?" She shivered again. "Could we talk about something else for a while?"

"Yes." William Edmonds smiled.

Tony held out the metal stud he had found outside their room the night before. Showing it around the table he asked, "Does anyone recognize this? Or know what it is?"

"Because *we* don't," Pat said.

Edmonds held his hand out, flat palm up, and Tony dropped the stud in it. "Hexagonal," he said. "Metal. Stainless steel?" With the tip of a fingernail he traced along the two metal prongs extending, slightly bent, from the flat side of the stud. "And these two arms that spread apart and hold it in place like a—" he snapped his fingers, trying to remember a term.

"A cotter pin," Tony said.

"Thank you. It looks like a decorative stud from a leather bag. Or a belt. Or jacket."

He swung his hand around to Donna who took the metal piece in her blunt, freckled fingers.

Edmonds looked at Tony. "Don't *you* know what it is?"

Tony shook his head. "I found it on the floor outside our room last night—outside *Shimada's* room."

The manager cocked his head. "Shouldn't the police have that?"

"They'll get it. In fact, you can give it to them if you want to."

Pat said, "It isn't ours."

Handing the stud back to Edmonds, Donna sounded like an echo when she said, "And it isn't ours."

Everybody paused. Tony looked away, Pat checked her fingernails, and Edmonds sipped coffee, each face blank and noncommittal. They sat through several moments of what might be called oddly embarrassed silence until Donna shook her head, shifting her frown into an almost condescending smile. "I mean," she said, "it isn't mine. And I don't think it belongs to Dennis."

Another, shorter silence was broken when Pat said, "Tony says that you've spent a lot of time in Japan."

"Yes."

"Long enough to learn that difficult language, I understand."

"My parents were missionaries. They took me to Japan in 1961, when I was four years old. I lived in Japan for fourteen years, enough time to learn the language. And much more. I was educated there.

"I learned what a lovely country it is, filled with lovely people—a people and culture to be respected. And preserved." Her pink lips moved in a small smile. "I like to think that I grew up there. Matured there."

Her expression turned cold again. "My parents died in 1975 and I came to America to live with an aunt, in

Colorado. I stayed three years and learned three things—to ride, to fish, to shoot. In three years, that's all this country could teach me.''

She paused and then, head up, chin out, she looked around the room and said, ''No. I also learned how shallow this society is. I went back to Japan to live. Happily.''

''What draws you there so strongly?'' Pat asked. ''What's the appeal?''

''As I said, Japan is filled with lovely people. Like Dennis. They're very strong, in many ways, but gentle, in many ways. They have real culture, which is something that Americans will never understand. Or appreciate.''

Pat shifted in her chair and opened her mouth but before she could respond William Edmonds asked her, ''Have you been to Japan?''

She looked at him, surprised. ''No.''

''I've been there twice—trips organized by the state's tourism specialists to help hotel and tour operators learn something about Japanese tourists.''

His earnest brown eyes looked at each person around the table as he spoke. ''My first reaction was, 'What an arrogant people!' But then I watched. And thought. And finally I realized, it's not arrogance, it's just that these are people who feel secure.'' He gestured toward the interpreter. ''As Donna says, they are a people very secure in their culture.''

Donna nodded. "And Dennis Shimada is a superior example of that culture. As such, he should be protected. While he's here—working in, exposed to, surrounded by this country's crude vulgarities—he must be protected from its corruption."

Her voice was cold, her face grim and pale. She leaned forward, intense, her hands curled shut into white-knuckled fists bouncing on the tabletop. "Dennis Shimada must be protected especially from that shallow farm girl and her cowboy—"

She stopped. Without another word she jumped up, grabbed her brown leather shoulder bag, and hurried out of the dining room.

Edmonds looked at her back as she left. Tony and Pat looked at each other.

THIRTY MINUTES LATER, sitting beside Tony in the Bronco, Pat rolled the passenger window part-way down and sniffed the scent of mint and sage and pine coming in on the blowing air.

"I've always wanted to see somebody making a movie or a TV show," she'd often said. So now she was riding along a blacktop county road on her way to see a TV crew shoot a staged cattle roundup.

Her head turned and her eyes moved constantly, watching the field, the fenceposts, the drooping powerlines, the sky. Several times she pointed to the black-and-white flutter of magpies flying over a field, to a red-tailed hawk standing stolid and vigilant on a fencepost. Once she whispered, "Listen," and through the rush of air Tony heard a meadowlark's song.

That was the only conversation. Pat and Tony had long since stopped trying to figure out Donna Hughes and her little scene at breakfast.

One opinion offered was that the interpreter had expressed the overwrought attitude of an expatriate trying to justify her attraction to a foreign country and the male inhabitants thereof.

On the other hand, Pat said, "I think she's a dippy broad."

They were fairly close behind a Chevy pickup and Tony was so surprised by her remark that he barely missed rear-ending the Chevy when it suddenly braked and snapped off a right turn road. "Wow." He flapped a hand at the truck angling away up a rugged side road trailing a cloud of dust. "Did you see that?"

"What? You almost drove up his tailpipe?"

"No. The sign on his side."

She looked again through the dust the truck stirred up and barely made out a small, square red-and-white magnetic sign stuck on the driver's door. "Good heavens. 'Explosives'!"

"How'd you like that for an after-breakfast treat?— a little taste of dynamite or who-knows-what."

"Where do you suppose he's going?"

"Don't know. I guess there's a logging crew working up there somewhere," and he waved toward the hills climbing up and away to the right.

"I thought trucks carrying explosives were supposed to have 'warning' signs up the ying-yang—back, front, sides, all over."

"I guess some of the folks around here get a little casual about that sort of thing."

So that was the end of the conversation for a while and Pat resumed her birdwatching.

About a quarter-mile after the truck incident, Tony turned right onto a gravel road running almost parallel to the track that the truck had taken. In fact, off to her right—against a dark background of pine trees— Pat saw a faint smudge of reddish dust drifting along a ledge where the truck might be traversing the high, wide hill.

The ledge was like a dividing line. Or a watermark. Above it, a forest of huge pines grew. Below it, only rocks and sagebrush and, in a few hillside folds, occasional junipers.

Tony stayed on the gravel road a few minutes, till the road forked. The gravel surface continued straight a little farther and then bent slowly in a gradual curve to the right around the rocky base of the hill that now crowded in.

The other fork was nothing but a rough dirt track jutting off to the left. Tony let the Bronco follow it slowly down and up through a shallow dip. On the other side, they came to a sagging barbed wire fence with a wide Z-frame wood gate, the wood weathered gray and black-veined. Pat tugged the gate open and closed and slung its rusty chain loop over the fence-post again. Then they jounced along a faint trail through sagebrush and mullein, over scruffy grass, red dirt, and rocks.

Finally they topped a gentle rise and suddenly— "out there in the middle of nowhere," according to Pat—there was the camera van. And on top stood the tall, thin cameraman in white Nikes, tan Levis, blue knit shirt and floppy white tennis hat. A long thin cigarette burned unnoticed between the first two fingers of his right hand while he hunched over the eyepiece on his tripod-mounted camera, panning right-to-left, back again, trying zooms, checking focus, keeping his moves smooth.

Tony parked the Bronco away from the van, leaving room for the van to maneuver in case the camera had to be repositioned in a hurry. Then he stood with Pat looking out over the location for this morning's shoot—the roundup scene.

About fifty yards in front of them, down a slight slope from the low ridge where they stood were two hundred head of white-faced brown cattle.

"Herefords?" Pat asked.

Tony nodded. Then he wrinkled his face in a "How should I know?" expression and shrugged.

Pat shook her head, once, and looked again to the scene in front of her in the little valley. The herd was directly ahead and spreading out to her left where she saw several people on horses, including a blonde girl and a small boy.

There were two cowboys on horseback riding beside the head of the herd, one just down the slope about fifty yards. Across the valley, perhaps two hundred yards away, the other cowboy rode along the foot of a rocky slope that rose past a few boulders to a rock outcropping just below the crest of the ridge.

The valley opened to the right and left. To the right it led between the two ridges to pastures. To the left, trails ran up to the Miller barnyard.

"This looks like a pretty good spot," Pat said. "They can only go one way or the other."

Arms folded across his chest, Tony bounced up on his toes once and said, "I thought so."

"Clever devil," she said, and then flinched as a sudden explosion cracked across the valley. "What was that!" She frowned, watching the two horses ahead of her doing a nervous little sideways dance.

"Probably those loggers." He touched her elbow and said, "Let's say hello to Nobu. You can take a look at the van."

Nobu was at the side of the van, where the doors were folded open, talking to someone inside. He leaned into the opening with his slender body arched forward, holding on to the top of the door frame with his right hand, fingers pinched into the rain gutter. His left hand wrapped around a walkie-talkie.

After a quick nod and smile to Tony and Pat, Nobu went back to his conversation in Japanese. Pat peeked around and past him.

He was talking to two assistants sitting on low stools on the bare metal floor of the van. Fitted into racks bolted to the floor in front of the stools were a video-tape recorder, a reel-to-reel tape recorder, and a color television monitor with a constantly changing picture. Hanging from hooks on the van walls, thick black cables and orange extension cords drooped down, coiled into big figure eights.

Pat looked at Tony, raised her eyebrows, and pointed to the picture on the monitor.

''That's from the cameraman on the roof. He's making sure everything works, no rough spots in the pans or zooms, stuff like that.''

At that moment the camera, and the picture on the monitor, panned from left to right and Pat saw the same view that she and Tony had been looking at just a few moments earlier—the people on horseback, the herd of white-faced brown cattle with the rocky hillside in the background, and the two cowboys, one of whom was still having trouble controlling his nervous horse.

Then the camera made a series of moves so quick and hard they made Pat dizzy—watching the monitor, she felt that her eyes were being yanked out of her head.

She saw a long, slow shot panning over the cattle and up the rocky brown hillside to some boulders on the crest, followed by a slow zoom in till one huge rock filled the screen and a zoom back till it was just a pebble on the hillside and then a sudden series of zooms in and out and in and out and in so that the rock seemed to be flying into her face and then flying away so fast that her eyes and brain couldn't keep up.

Pat was about to close her eyes and turn away but the violent movement stopped. The picture slid down to the cattle and a leisurely panning shot, moving left, over what seemed to be a sea of shifting brown hides dotted with large round pink eyes.

The camera ended that move by picking out the people on horseback at the rear of the herd—the boy, Norio Sakata; the handsome Japanese actor, Dennis Shimada; the cowboy, JayDee Hampton, and the pretty young girl, Jo Miller. They faced the camera, far away and unaware as it closed in, centering on the girl and her pink T-shirt and blue jeans.

Continuing in, it moved past her horse's head, gliding toward the girl till her face filled the screen, short blonde hair drifting in the breeze, smiling blue eyes fixed on the handsome actor.

Now the camera came even closer. It focused on her full pink lips, watched them moving in silent conversation. It panned down her slender suntanned neck.

Finally, the flat screen filled with her round, swelling, pink left breast.

Inside the van, silence fell on Nobu and his assistants. They admired the camera work for several seconds before Nobu glanced at Pat, then leaned back and shouted up to the cameraman. Immediately, the picture on the monitor became a large brown cow. It flinched as another explosion boomed over the little valley.

Nobu stepped away from the van and looked around, hands on hips. "Tono-san?"

"I think it's a logging crew way up there in the woods, to the right. Clearing a road or something."

The walkie-talkie radio in Nobu's hand let out two quick spurts of static but he paid no attention. Instead, he stepped away from the van, frowning. He looked all around, past the van to the people in the valley, back to Tony's Bronco, down the trail. "Donna is not here?"

"I haven't seen her since breakfast."

Still frowning, Nobu said, "Where is interpreter when needed? Ha?"

His radio crackled again, two shorts bursts of static asking for attention. This time he held it up and pressed the contact twice to signal. "Go ahead."

From his position at the rear of the herd, the assistant director's high-pitched voice came over the noisy little radio. In a series of abrupt Japanese phrases he told his director that the riders were ready, the cattle were ready, and he was ready. Everyone was ready to start moving the cattle.

Nobu's answer was a quiet *"Hai,"* meaning "Yes." He shouted something to the cameraman and got back another, *"Hai!"* The picture on the monitor suddenly focused on the ground just ahead of the lead cattle's hooves.

Looking into the van, Nobu gave the cue to start the recording tape. He spoke loudly across his radio mouthpiece, making sure the tape operator in the van heard him as well as the assistant director at the other walkie-talkie. *"Mawashite!"*

The blank tape on the video recorder started rolling. The reels made about four revolutions before the operator shouted, *"Mawatta."* The tape was up to speed, rolling smoothly, ready to record.

Nobu waited one more second before he gave the cue for action. And when he gave it, it wasn't very dramatic. He said, "Start."

NINE

Friday (continued)

IMMEDIATELY AFTER Nobu's cue, Pat heard shouts and whistles in the distance. Some cattle bawled. She looked at the monitor in time to see why the cameraman had focused on that patch of dirt just ahead of the herd.

A tight close-up showed one big hoof after another clomping down in a puff of dust before the lens pulled back a little for a wider shot and she saw the lead cattle beginning to move the herd to the right, down the valley toward the pass.

Pat wanted to see more, to compare the entire scene with the pictures she saw on the monitor. She backed away from the van a few steps and stood in front of Tony, holding one hand above her eyes like a sun visor. From there she could see the monitor inside the truck and, by turning her head a little, she could also see all of the action being photographed.

The cowboys at the head of the herd rode on each side of the front ranks, leading or guiding them down the valley to her right. The riders behind the herd rode to and fro, urging the cattle forward.

It was slow going at first. Most of the cattle wouldn't move till those in the back rows crowded those ahead who crowded those ahead and so on up to the front of the herd. But, once started, they ambled down the valley. "Just as though they knew where they were going," Pat said over her shoulder to Tony.

He stood behind her looking over her head, his hands on her shoulders, his thumbs gently kneading the back of her neck. He nodded while he looked back and forth between the action in the valley and its moving picture on the monitor. "Yes," he said. "Nobu seems happy with it, too."

The director leaned into the van, intense, his hands spread flat on the floor. He muttered half to himself and half to his assistants, concentrating on the monitor, bobbing his head up and down as the cameraman repeatedly zoomed, panned, and framed close-ups of different sections of the plodding herd. Finally, after about five minutes, Nobu straightened and stepped back. He looked up at the cameraman. "Cut-oh!" he called out. The screen went black.

He spoke quickly into his radio, at the same time pointing to one of the men in the van. The man jumped out, ran around the van, clambered up into the driver's seat and, after a couple of seconds, the engine roared. Pat, watching the cattle, saw a couple of heads jerk up, looking in her direction.

Nobu yelled to the cameraman, who hunched over his eyepiece, flexed his knees, and twisted his feet

slightly as though trying to screw them into the platform on top of the van.

The van began moving carefully. Pat and Tony
walked alongside with Nobu. On the roof, the cameraman started shooting again.

In the herd, by this time, more long white-faced
heads raised up, held high and alert, some bawling
nervously, stretching and swinging around trying to
watch the van rolling slowly down the gentle slope,
coming a little closer. It was pointing toward the rear
of the herd, changing the camera angle from a profile
to a rear three-quarter shot.

From up in the hills another explosion boomed and
rolled across the valley.

The van stopped after about fifty feet. The monitor inside showed a wide-angle shot of cattle rumps—
as Pat put it, "the south end of a lot of northbound
cows." They lumbered toward a pass between the
rocky hillside on the left and the bare hills leading up
to the forest on the right.

Nobu spoke into his radio. The actor Shimada and
the young boy rode into the edge of the scene. Nobu
spoke again. Shimada guided both horses to the right.
Nobu spoke again, to the cameraman overhead and to
the radio. The camera angle narrowed slightly. Now
Shimada and the boy, looking straight ahead and riding side-by-side on the bottom-center of the frame,
seemed to be driving the herd toward the pass.

Pat looked away from the monitor to the actual scene. The girl and the cowboy rode on either side of the actors, apparently just out of camera range. Two other riders rode at the edge of the herd.

Another dynamite blast roared into the valley, and one of the horses reared and almost dumped its rider.

The cattle in front slowed. A few began turning to the right, a few to the left, trying to go back in the direction they'd come from. Some stopped. The cattle coming behind bumped into those ahead. The quiet, docile herd was becoming a milling, bawling mess. Eyes rolled and horns clattered against horns as they pushed, shoved, butted each other to get away from the lead cowboys coming to get them under control and moving in one direction again.

At that moment another, bigger explosion boomed into the valley and the entire herd began wheeling to follow the leaders, in a panic, out of all control, swirling, pawing, climbing all over each other.

Tony grabbed Pat. "Get in the van. Stay there."

Nobu was yelling into his radio but Tony yelled louder, pointing to the men in the valley. "Tell your crew to run this way." Nobu nodded. Tony jabbed a thumb over his shoulder at the hill the van had just come down. "Take the van back up?" Nobu nodded again and Tony ran for the Bronco.

"Where're you *going*?" Pat shouted at his back.

"After the boy. And the people on foot."

Tony gunned the Bronco down the shallow slope. It wasn't much of a rise but he hit the valley floor so hard that he felt the Bronco's suspension flatten and thump.

Tromping on the pedal he raced for the opening between the riders and the herd, a lane about twenty yards wide with the herd on his right and the riders coming toward him on his left—the boy in front followed by Dennis Shimada, Jo Miller, and JayDee Hampton. To the left of the riders, the assistant director and two other cameraman ran toward him, too, but on foot.

Nearly all of the herd had now turned completely around, a few already running toward the riders, closing the lane between them. Jo and the others seemed slow in getting out of the way, possibly because two of them—Norio and Dennis—were not experienced riders and none of the horses was a real Derby winner.

Suddenly, the boy dropped his reins and wrapped his hands around his saddlehorn. Jo saw him holding on for dear life, and she spurred ahead. Grabbing his loose reins, she charged on, pulling the other horse.

Behind Shimada, JayDee's mare screamed and stumbled. Her forelegs collapsed. JayDee kicked free of the stirrups. She crashed into the ground as he slid out of the saddle. She rolled up onto her right shoulder, tail in the air, hooves flailing. He landed running, straw hat flying behind, but he stumbled and skidded headfirst through the dirt beside his mare. She finished her roll-over, legs thrashing the air, and barely missed crushing him into the dirt as she smashed down full length with a screaming grunt and then lay with a foreleg twitching in a rising cloud of dust.

One foot from his horse JayDee lay still and quiet, facedown in the dirt.

Tony hit the brakes just as Jo came racing back past him screaming, "JayDee! JayDee!"

"What the hell is she coming back *here* for?" The thought flashed through Tony's mind and he glanced over his shoulder. Behind him, the boy and Shimada seemed on their way to safety across the valley floor.

Now, to his right, the cattle were in a full-scale stampede, two-hundred brown bodies heaving, white-faced heads rocking up and down, big dull eyes oddly intent as sharp hooves cut the distance toward Jo, who had jumped down and now knelt by JayDee's body. She held her own horse's reins in one hand, her back to the stampeding cattle.

Hoping to split the onrushing herd, to use his Bronco like a wedge in front of the herd and force it to divide and go around JayDee and Jo, Tony hit the brakes and slid to a stop a few feet behind her. Her frightened horse, trying to look back at the cattle, danced and jittered around and almost trampled JayDee.

Focused on the herd and on Jo, Tony hadn't seen the pickup truck tearing across the valley floor from the other direction. But suddenly there was Gramp

Miller. Bouncing around in the cab of his truck, his thick stubby forearms and hands surrounding the steering wheel, the tense little old man bore down to save his granddaughter.

He swung his truck into a skid that nearly rammed the Bronco's grill before it stopped, but the two made a V-shaped barricade that did what Tony'd hoped for—the herd split, flowing around and past Jo and JayDee like a river flowing around a boulder.

Gramp's move saved more than Jo and JayDee. The three TV crewmen were able to duck into the protective V instead of trying to outrun the herd.

But the next thing Gramp did was almost fatal for Jo.

She still knelt in the dust beside JayDee, ignoring the frightening uproar all around her, sheltering his scratched and bleeding face in her arms. Gramp tried everything he could think of to drive the thundering herd away from his granddaughter. He waved his hat out the window, he yelled, and he hit the horn in long, loud blasts.

He was trying to help Jo but he terrified her horse which was already close to panic. Surrounded by stampeding, bellowing cattle, feeling the ground shaking under his feet, seeing another horse stretched out on the ground, Jo's horse heard the blaring horn and went wild. He rolled his eyes and quivered all over and his head jerked up and yanked his reins out of Jo's hand.

The tug pulled her off balance. She started to fall across JayDee's body as her horse reared. His right front foot swung up and cracked her in the ribs and when his foot came back down its shoe scraped the skin behind her right ear, coming that close to crushing her skull. He skittered and pranced around and by some miracle missed trampling both Jo and JayDee as he turned and raced for the barn with the cattle, trailing his reins in the dirt.

Tony and Gramp hurried toward Jo as the rest of the herd rushed past.

Jo wrapped one arm around her stomach, clutching her side. With her other hand she pushed herself back up to her knees again. JayDee was sitting up, too, rubbing his head and looking at Jo. Then they both turned to his horse.

Jo crawled over to the mare. On her knees, she stroked the hores's back and neck with her free hand as she inched along past the saddle to the quiet head. There she suddenly stopped and jerked her hand away, shuddering. A harsh rasping sound grated deep in her throat and she rocked back on her heels. She turned her bloodshot eyes and pale, dirty, sweat-streaked face to JayDee, then Tony, then Gramp before looking down at the mare again. "Dead," she whispered. "Shot." She looked at JayDee. "How . . . ?"

LATER THAT MORNING there were few outward signs that anything unusual had happened.

One indication was the sight of Pat pacing back and forth outside the camera van and kicking every rock, twig, leaf, and bug that crossed her path. And every time she kicked she muttered, "Tony!"

Another was that she kept muttering things like, "Who the hell does he think he is, Buffalo Bill?" And, "A man your age should never chase cows. You embarrass the children." And, "Are you trying to make me a widow?"

There was almost a thin blue plume of smoke curling out of each ear.

Otherwise, things seemed pretty well in hand. Gramp had taken Jo and JayDee to the hospital "just for a look-see," as he put it, even though they both told him "not to make a federal case out of a few scratches."

The other riders got the cattle settled down and grazing comfortably not far from the barnyard.

The three crewmen who'd been on foot in the path of the stampede were calmer now. They each came up to the equipment truck, filled a paper cup with iced tea, and sat down behind the truck in the shade, chain-smoking cigarettes and dropping the butts in their tea.

JayDee's dead mare, however, was still stretched out on the valley floor. Gramp had wanted to winch her onto a flatbed and haul her away. However, Tony suggested that the sheriff might want her left "as is, until the crime scene investigators get a look at her. If they have crime scene investigators out here. And if they investigate the scene of a horse shooting."

That idea was "just a hair this side of stupid," in Gramp's opinion, but he agreed to stop by the sheriff's office on his way back from taking Jo and JayDee to the hospital.

So now—while Pat marched around outside—Tony sat inside the camera van, slumped crosslegged on the floor in front of the monitor. Beside him, sitting on low stools, Nobu and one of his technicians watched replays of the roundup footage as they checked and timed scenes to use in the show.

They were down to the last of the three-quarter-angle long shots showing the herd and the rocky hillside in the background, with Shimada and the boy riding into the scene. The camera held them in the frame for about fifteen seconds before both actors looked left, nodded, and rode left out of the picture. Apparently they were getting into position for another take because the tape kept rolling and the camera stayed on.

But the cameraman, as usual, kept his camera moving. Pan of the herd. Zoom up to the hills. Back to the herd. And then the picture bounced, went out of focus, in again. Tony sat up. "I wonder if that was the big explosion."

On the monitor, the herd milled and turned. The camera whipped left and the picture blurred and then on popped Jo, JayDee, Shimada, and the boy, all looking scared. Jo and JayDee, their mouths wide open, whipped and kicked at their horses' flanks, turning toward the camera-side of the valley. Yelling and waving, they were trying to get Shimada and the boy turned, too. Confused, the two spun their horses completely around before they started to the side.

Tony shook his head. "Don't tell me I get to re-live that whole thing!"

Suddenly the picture changed, like a cut, to a close-up of the herd. Then it moved down to the running hooves churning dust. Up to the cattle's wild-eyed faces. Pulled back to a wide shot of the herd. Panned left, with the hillside in the background and Tony straightened. "Stop!"

The technician jabbed the stop button and the picture froze on a blur of running cattle.

Tony pointed to the monitor and slapped Nobu's arm with the back of his other hand. "Did you see that?"

"Excuse? See what, Tono-san?"

Tony waved his hand in a circle. "Roll it back. Look at it again. Maybe *I* didn't see it." He rocked up on his knees, closer to the monitor.

The tape rewound about ten turns, started forward, and once again the camera panned over the stampeding cattle and the hillside. "There! Stop it!"

The picture froze, cattle in mid-stride. The two other men looked at Tony.

He held out his hands, fingers splayed and pointing down. He twisted his hands counter-clockwise.
"Roll it back by hand. Five or six turns."

Nobu started to translate but the technician had already reached for the recording machine. He snapped
the "record" gate open and began rewinding the tape
manually.

On the monitor, the herd of cattle jerked backwards two steps and stopped. Nobu leaned forward
beside Tony. Another two steps and stop. Another two
steps and—"Stop! There!"

Tony sat on his heels in front of the monitor and
tapped the glass with his index finger. "See?" Against
the background of a small stand of junipers, a little
blue cloud had suddenly popped out on the rocky
hillside just above a cluster of boulders.

Nobu shook his head, not believing what he saw.
Softly he said, "Smoke?" He spoke rapid Japanese to
his assistant, who gave a negative shrug but a positive
nod and rewound the tape once more.

The machine clicked and whirred, the wheels
turned, the cattle started running again, the camera
panned, and there on the hillside the puff appeared.

"Oh, no, Tono-san. Gunshot?"

A gruff voice from the doorway blurted, "Gunshot! What're you talkin' about. Gunshot?"

Tony looked around and saw a short, heavyset man
squinting into the truck, one hand shading his eyes
from the sun that made his badge sparkle on his chest.

"Hey, 'Coop,'" Tony said. "Climb on in here," and he held out a hand to help Barlow County Sheriff Eldon Cooper into the van. After introducing Sheriff Cooper to Nobu Tony asked, "Did Gramp Miller talk to you?"

"Why else would I be out here instead of in my air-conditioned office? What's this about a dead horse? And where's that gunshot you were just talkin' about?"

Tony explained what he'd seen on the tape, or what he *thought* he'd seen. "So the horse was shot, and we may have a picture of gunsmoke." He motioned for another tape replay. "Now, watch the monitor and *you* tell *us*," he said.

"High tech detecting, huh?" The sheriff sounded slightly sarcastic. But after watching the tape a couple of times he said, "Well sort o' looks like that to me, too."

"And maybe," Tony added, "maybe the shooter wasn't shooting at the horse. Maybe he meant to hit JayDee."

The sheriff's dark brown eyes turned very serious. "I'll take a look at that horse and then go up there and see what I can see."

"Mind if I come along?"

"Fine with me."

Tony hopped out of the van and almost bumped into Pat, who had stopped marching up and down and was leaning against the open door. "Well, Mr. Dillon," she said through her teeth, "where are we off to now? Dodge City?"

He put an arm around her shoulders and they walked slowly along the side of the van. "What's wrong?"

"Where are you going?"

"I'm just going with the sheriff to—"

"That's what's wrong." She stopped so he stopped. "How many other police officers have told you, quote, Mr. Pratt, stay out of it, unquote. Mr. Pratt, leave police work to police officers, unquote."

"Right. You're right. Sergeant Kelsey said that."

"Quote, your insurance isn't paid up and your royalties aren't enough for your widow and two children to live extremely well on, unquote."

"Who said that?"

"I said that. And I say give it up. Let the sheriff—"

"Pat." He pointed to the hillside across the little valley. "We're just going over there to look around those rocks."

"Why?"

"Because we think that's where the shot came from that killed the horse."

Pat looked across at the rocks. "So you think somebody was up there with a gun." He nodded.

"And shot the horse." He nodded again. "And that's where you want to go."

"Yes."

"Not . . . too . . . bright."

TEN

PAT TOOK the keys to the Bronco to drive back to The Lodge. "I, for one, am getting out of this heat," she said. "And you should come with me."

"No, I'm going with the sheriff," he said. "Think of this as research."

She pressed her palm against his forehead. "I think you've been out in the sun too long."

He pulled her hand down and kissed it. "Stop worrying."

"Wear a hat."

"Yes."

"Did you bring a hat?"

"No. Stop worrying. Drive carefully."

After Pat left, Tony slid into a tan Barlow County Jeep alongside Sheriff Cooper and they drove over to JayDee Hampton's dead horse, still stretched out on the valley floor.

While Tony leaned against the door of the Jeep, against the yellow and green Barlow County logo, the sheriff walked a couple of times around JayDee's mare. He squatted down by her head, sitting on his heels, brushing the flies away with a rough, heavy hand. He pushed his straw hat back off his forehead and squinted up at the hillside.

He stood and walked a few feet from the horse's body, studying the dusty ground. He stopped, pointing down. More to himself than to Tony, Cooper said, "Here's where she dropped." He moved again. Stopped again. Nodded, "Mmm-hmm. Must've got hit about here."

Cooper turned and once more squinted at the hillside, seeming to measure the distance to the stand of junipers and the rocks just below.

"If that shooter aimed for JayDee, he didn't do too good. If he aimed for the horse, though, he did pretty slick, gettin' her right behind the ear."

The sheriff grunted, getting up. "We'll have to get that bullet outa there and see what it came from."

In the Jeep again, Sheriff Cooper drove to the end of the valley where a faint two-wheel track led up the rocky spine of the hill. He shifted into low. Kicking up the rugged trail, the Jeep creaked and rattled over the rocks while Tony and the sheriff bounced around inside, saying nothing.

Along the crest they passed several rock outcroppings and a few isolated oaks before they came to the stand of junipers they were looking for, cupped in a shallow bowl just below the trail on the right. Cooper pulled up in the shadow of the trees and Tony got out.

The first thing he noticed was the silence. He turned his head from side to side, listening. The only sound was the soft breathing of wind through the trees, as if the whole wide blue sky were filled with nothing but sunlight and quiet. He saw Cooper watching him, a little smile on his round face. "Sounds good, don't it?" the sheriff said.

The next thing Tony noticed stopped him cold. Cooper came around the car and Tony pointed to the base of one of the junipers where something had chewed up the dirt. Cooper nodded. "Somebody must've tied his horse up there for a good little time."

They circled to get around the tracks and go through the trees but Tony stopped again.

"Look at that." A small puddle of oil stained a tuft of grass beside the trail.

Cooper glanced down. "Prob'ly from one of the Miller trucks. Win or Gramp or somebody. Prob'ly stopped to take a leak or something."

Tony stood by the trail looking at the ground all around. He crossed the narrow road. "There's another one," he said. He walked back along the trail a few steps and stopped. "Here."

The sheriff walked over and stood beside Tony, looking down at a wide, long oval where oil had stained the dirt and scruffy clumps of grass and seeped into the soil. Cooper shook his head. "Must've tore off his oil pan or something. Let's go."

Tony looked up the hill at the lava outcroppings and sage and sparse grass before he followed the sheriff back across the trail and through the trees.

There they stopped and studied the rocks ten feet down the slope.

Two big flat-topped boulders sat side-by-side on a short, wide shelf. Their squat black shadows bulged out over the bare trackless rock. Half-hidden by the rock and shadow, an empty cartridge caught just enough sunlight for Tony and the sheriff to spot it at the same time.

They both started to point, then Cooper walked over to it and bent down. When he straightened, he held the empty casing on the end of a ballpoint pen and it rattled a little as he walked carefully around looking at the ground, at the rocks, and out over the valley. Every few seconds he'd stop and say something out loud, whether to himself or to Tony it was hard to tell. But Tony listened.

"We've got a team of crime scene investigators and I could call 'em up here.

"But I'm not sure I've got a crime.

"What I've got is a dead horse, which is bad enough." Sheriff Cooper turned his head and looked at Tony. "But if the shooter was aimin' at the rider, that's a totally different story." He turned away, squinting toward JayDee's mare on the valley floor. "Funny thing, though..."

He stopped and his pause went on and on till Tony said, "What's that?"

"Most people around here don't mess with guns. But the ones that do, they can handle a rifle pretty well. Some can even knock the knob off a gnat's pecker." He looked at Tony again. "Pretty unusual to aim at a rider and hit his horse."

Cooper started up the slope toward his Jeep. Tony turned to go with him but Cooper stopped him in his tracks with a bitter laugh. "Y'know, Tony, when you came in a few weeks ago to introduce yourself and tell me that you'd have these television people workin' around here, you never told me you'd be taking pictures of a shooting."

"No." Tony had a grim smile on his face. "That's one possibility that never even occurred to me."

They passed the junipers again and the sheriff jerked a thumb toward the scuffed-up ground where the horse had been tethered. "I could rope this off," he said, "but I seriously doubt that there's gonna be one whole helluva lot o' people walkin' through here."

At his car, Cooper took a plastic bag out of the glove box, dropped the empty cartridge inside, and put the bag back.

Tony leaned against the Jeep's dusty right rear fender, looking through the trees toward the boulders and on to the valley. The sheriff closed the glove box and started around to the driver's side, but he stopped beside Tony. "What's on your mind?"

"Wondering who'd shoot at JayDee. And why. And if they weren't shooting at JayDee, which of the others was the target? And why?" He shrugged. "Naturally, I don't know much *about* him, just what I've heard in the short time I've been here. Does he have any enemies or—"

Cooper snorted. "At one time or another"—he turned and leaned his bulky back against the Jeep, folding his arms across his chest. His added weight made the Jeep shift a little so that Tony had to shift a little, too—"at one time or another, just about everybody in town over the age of four's wanted to kick JayDee's ass. Then they usually have second thoughts, real quick, and remember who he is and what he came from. So then they cool off and nothing happens. Usually."

Tony opened his mouth to ask a question but the sheriff asked one first. "A minute ago you were wondering: 'If they weren't shootin' at JayDee—who?' You tell me. Who else was down there on the valley floor close to him?"

"Four people. On horseback. Jo Miller. JayDee. And two of the Japanese actors—the young boy and the man named Shimada."

"'Shi-ma-da'? That how you pronounce it?"

"Dennis Shimada."

Sheriff Cooper's head tilted back and he slowly scratched at his Adam's apple a couple of times. "He's the one JayDee had a run-in with? About Jo?"

Tony's eyebrows popped up. "How'd you know about that?"

Cooper glanced at Tony before a quick smile moved across his face. "This TV show you're making—to you, I guess, it's just a job. But nobody around here's ever seen anything like it. It's got everybody all excited. They talk about everything you people do. Word gets around.''

With a little grunt and a nudge of his shoulders, Cooper pushed himself away from the Jeep and stood up straight, stretching. ''So. You say there were four people on the valley floor when the horse got shot. Where were you?''

''Me? I was with the camera van, up there on that little ridge where it is now. Until the stampede started.''

''Then what?''

''I drove the Bronco down to try to head off the herd.''

''When did the horse go down?''

''During the stampede.''

The sheriff took a few steps to his left, talking as he walked. ''So you were there, too. When the horse got shot.''

''I'll be damned.'' Tony stood up straight. ''It happened so fast I didn't even think of it that way.'' He shook his head and followed Cooper. ''You're right. I was there, too.''

Looking through the trees, through the narrow gap in the rocks, down to the valley and JayDee's dead mare, the sheriff said, ''And from this angle, it seems to me, *you* were in the line of fire, too. So the shooter might've been shooting at you.''

Tony stared at him. The hillside became very quiet again. "That's crazy."

Cooper stared back. "That's what I think every time I hear about somebody gettin' shot."

"Why would anybody shoot at me?" Tony sounded dazed.

The sheriff's first answer was a tired shrug and a wag of his head before he said, "Why would anybody shoot at anybody?" Then his eyes narrowed, studying Tony's face. "You look like you could use a little rest. Let's get out of here so you can get back to The Lodge."

They didn't say another word while the sheriff wrestled his Jeep through a cramped U-turn on the ridge and got them bumping back down the narrow rocky track.

Tony broke his thoughtful silence. "You mentioned The Lodge and got me to wondering—maybe I'm mixed up in Dennis Shimada's problems. Somebody at The Lodge mentioned it this morning. Or maybe I've got a serious problem of my own, for some reason, and don't even know it."

"You talkin' about the snakes?"

Tony stared at him as much as the bouncing car allowed. "Now how the hell did you know about *that!* What do you people use out here in the country— jungle drums?"

Cooper laughed and said, "No, just the standard forms of communication. The telephone. The coffee shop. The tavern."

Shaking his head, Tony went on with his thoughts. "So you know about the snakes. Well. Whether meant for me *or* Shimada, a rattlesnake is a deadly weapon, right?"

"Could be."

"So what we're talking about is attempted murder, right?"

"Did you report it?"

"The Tribal Police were called."

"But you're talking about a possible felony. They don't have jurisdiction in the case of a felony. Even on the reservation."

"Is that right?"

Cooper quickly raised a cautioning finger. "I didn't say it was right. I just said that's the way it *is*."

Tony studied his profile for a few moments. "Okay, the reservation is in your county, right?" Cooper nodded and Tony went on. "Right. So I'm reporting it to you, the County Sheriff."

"Wrong. Wrong jurisdiction again. A felony on the reservation brings in the Bureau of Indian Affairs, which brings in the FBI."

"Jeez!" Tony said, commenting as much on the bump as they hit the valley floor as on the conversation. "Seems to me that you have a lot of different law enforcement agencies covering the same territory."

"Not really. Different agencies enforce different laws in different parts of it."

"Jurisdictions ever overlap?"

"Sometimes."

"What happens then?"

"We manage to cooperate. Generally."

After a moment, Tony smiled and said, "With all these lawmen around, what's the best approach?"

Sheriff Cooper glanced at him. "Stay out of trouble," he said, easing up on the accelerator as they once again drew near the body of the dead horse. He drove quietly past it, steadily turning his head to study it in a slow, calculating manner.

Once past, he kept driving at the same slow pace, now looking straight ahead with a sad, solemn expression on his face. "Losin' that mare's sure gonna be hard on JayDee." He shook his head. "She must've been about the only thing that anybody ever gave that boy."

ELEVEN

Saturday

U.S. HIGHWAY 97 becomes more of a highway when it meets Conroy, Oregon (Pop. 2,119). Suddenly, for eight blocks, that narrow little sliver of road metamorphoses into Main Street—two lanes north and two lanes south with a weedy concrete planter running ankle-high down the middle and a flashing yellow light above the Safeway entrance at the south end. Through-traffic doesn't slow down much for Conroy.

Still, the local people stopped and gawked every time the TV production company drove through town. At seven-forty-five on Saturday morning, of course, there weren't many people on Main. Even so, the ones that were there honked, waved a hand, or waggled a straw hat as the crew bus, the two-ton equipment truck, the camera van, and especially the station wagon full of actors went whooshing by.

At the end of the caravan—"bringing up the rear," she called it—Pat Pratt sat in the Ford Bronco beside her husband Tony. She also told him, "I feel as though we're riding behind the elephants with a broom and a scooper."

But the Bronco left the parade at Potter Street, turning at the Coast-to-Coast store, while the rest of the caravan continued on toward Nine Mountain Lake. At Pat's insistence, Tony and Pat were going to the hospital to see Jo Miller. It turned out that Gramp Miller had been right in taking his granddaughter Jo and JayDee to the hospital for a checkup after the stampede. JayDee, with just a few scratches on his forehead and left cheek from skidding through the dirt, had been released. Jo, on the other hand, was in bed with a couple of cracked ribs and a very stiff neck.

During dinner last night, Pat had suggested stopping to see Jo on the way through town. Tony'd agreed. "But the thing is," he'd said, "tomorrow we're shooting the rafting sequence on the river, just below Nine Mountain Lake. So we'll be leaving early—too early for visiting hours."

"You're forgetting that this is a small town. I grew up in a small town. Small town hospitals don't have the same narrow rules that city hospitals have. You just go when you can get there."

"Okay, we'll give it a shot."

"Good." She dropped her napkin beside her plate. "Let's find her a little present in the gift shop before we go upstairs."

A smile pulled at the corners of his mouth as he came around to help with her chair. "Speaking of upstairs..."

She looped her purse strap over her shoulder and said quietly. "That's a very suspicious expression on your face."

"I was just looking forward to a little dessert. Or something." Turning from the table, he let one hand graze her seersucker slacks as she started toward the door.

She stopped, gazing at him over her shoulder. "Why, Mister Dillon. After playing with your cows all day, are you trying to tell me that you still have juices jangling?"

"Miss Kitty, when I look at you, all I can see is that little room o' yours upstairs over the Long Branch."

"You romantic devil, you."

So, early Saturday morning, there they were—Pat with a gift for Jo, Tony with a trace of a smile on his face—walking into the Barlow County Hospital.

The cream-colored brick building was one story tall. It had tan tile floors that gleamed, cool white walls, and a casually competent feel about it. And, as Pat had said, visiting hours seemed to be what you wanted them to be. In fact, they passed two or three couples who were leaving, their morning visits already over.

They found Jo Miller in a corner room at the end of the hall. At first glance, the room seemed as cheerful and full of light as a hospital room can be. But when they saw Jo, Tony and Pat sensed a gloom that nearly froze them into silence, and Pat whispered, "There's a girl who needs a friend."

She was alone in the two-bed room, in the bed beside the window. With her head and shoulders propped up by pillows and her face turned toward the early morning sun, they first saw her in dramatic, cameo-like partial profile. Her short red-blonde hair and outdoor complexion looked vigorous, young, and alive in the fresh morning light from the window. But that same light put black shadows in the furrows between her brows. Her bright gray eyes, usually filled with twenty-year-old life and sparkle, seemed sad and dark, old with worry and pain.

To Pat, Jo seemed to be looking beyond the far, snow-covered mountains, searching into the morning, watching this new day and hoping it would bring somebody who'd tell her that her troubles were over.

Even after Jo saw them, even after they tapped on the open door asking, "May we come in?"—even after they entered smiling and bringing gifts—her sad expression didn't change for several seconds.

She managed a small, polite smile for Pat and her self-styled "Care Package": a small packet of Aplets and Cotlets, a tin of Almond Roca, and the most recent issue of Vogue.

("Vogue!" Tony had said, "in Conroy?" Pat's answer was, "She lives in the country, not in a cave.")

Jo forced another smile when she opened Tony's card and sniffed the yellow rose he'd brought. But she seemed tense, nervous, and close to tears. She did little more than glance at Tony and she looked directly at Pat only once or twice.

Pauses in the conversation got longer and longer and Tony was about to wind things up when Pat said to Jo, "After meeting Gramp, I'm looking forward to meeting your father."

Jo took a quick breath and turned to the window again without saying anything.

So Pat added, "If he comes to see you this morning, I hope it's while we're still here."

There was another silence before Jo said quietly, "Gramp's coming. He's just pulling in. I don't think Daddy'll be here. I guess"—she stopped and then hurried on—"I guess his back's pretty bad."

Pat said, "Oh, he's hurt? I'm sorry. I didn't know." She looked at Tony, who was frowning and shaking his head.

Jo noticed and said flatly, "That's all right." She turned her head to Pat. "Daddy hurt his back in the accident that killed Momma." She glanced at Tony. "Five years ago. If I can't talk about it now, I'll never be able to."

She turned back to Pat. "A load of hay bales fell on her. Daddy hurt his back trying to pull 'em off and save her but it didn't do any good." Absently, she picked up the greeting card and put it back in its envelope. "He must've hurt himself really bad because it's bothered him ever since." She turned her head toward the window and her eyes searched the morning again. "Gramp says he's not sure which hurts Daddy more. His back or thinking that it was his fault Momma died 'cause he turned the wagon too sharp and the bales fell on her."

Now she looked straight at Pat. "Either way, he's been hurtin' for years and I don't know what to do." She squeezed her eyes shut and closed her mouth in a grim line. She clamped her teeth together so hard that she made muscles in her jaws bulge and move. Still, a few tears got away and rolled down her cheeks. She shook her head angrily and her hair tossed around her face and pillow.

Pat reached for Jo's hand and at the same time jerked a tissue out of the box on the bed tray. Without a word, she perched on the side of the bed and wiped the tears away from Jo's eyes, smoothing her hair away from her face.

After a few quick, shallow breaths Jo looked at Pat again and when she spoke the words spilled out as though she couldn't keep them in any longer. "Then last year JayDee showed up again and when he started working for us everything seemed to get better for a while. For Daddy and all. For a few months, anyway. But then Daddy got worse again. Some days he'd just lay around, or wander off in a daze somewhere."

She'd been holding Pat's hand, telling her story only to Pat. Now she suddenly pulled away for some reason and her eyes fired a mean, hard look at Tony. "Then you started coming around and JayDee got all nervous and jumpy and Daddy got worse. What are you looking for? What're you after?" She frowned and her eyes shifted sideways at Pat, suspicious. "Do you do the same kind of work *he* does?"

Surprised by the odd question, Pat glanced at Tony and he shrugged as if to say, "What's she talking about?" But then Pat's face relaxed in a dry little smile and she patted Jo's hand. "To tell you the truth," she said, "sometimes I don't even *know* what he does."

She stood up and just then Gramp's thin, high-pitched voice broke in from the doorway. "I'll swear, Jo-Jo, you're gettin' to be just like that JayDee—thinking *every*body's some kind of suspicious person."

"Oh, Gramp!" Jo said roughly, but she laughed when he hunched over with his hands behind him and stalked into the room like a conspirator, changing his voice to a loud, comical whisper. "Who's that over there? D'you know this guy over here? Who's that comin' down the trail? You ever seen this guy before?"

At Jo's bedside he straightened. "Here," he said, and from behind his back he presented a long, beautiful blue peacock feather.

Jo took the feather, smiling at the old man as he turned to Tony and Pat. He spoke in his gruff voice but, at the same time, he reached out with the fingers of his right hand and, with just the tips, he shyly, tenderly touched his granddaughter's hair, her shoulder, her arm. "Anybody can give a girl flowers, and no offense to the one that brought that yellow rose. But only a real, natural-born, high-quality sport brings a girl a peacock feather."

Bending, Gramp quickly popped a kiss on the top of Jo's head. "And take that, too." Still bent over he added, "But if you don't want it you have to give it back," and Jo smiled again and kissed his cheek.

"Good," Gramp said. "Now." He stood up and looked around the room. "Seen your daddy?"

Jo's face turned grim. "Haven't seen him." She raised the peacock feather upright between her thumb and index finger, twirling it, watching it. After a worried glance at Gramp she spun the feather some more. "Think he's back at the caves?"

Gramp's answer was a frowning shrug and another question. "JayDee?"

"Here and gone. Said he was—"

"Say anything about Win?"

Jo shook her head and went on, "—said he was going to the river." She looked at Pat and Tony and added, "Said the TV people were puttin' a raft in the water today and he wanted to see how long they'd last."

Tony tried to smile but it didn't work, so he just put a hand on Pat's shoulder and said, "Right. And I ought to get on over there, too."

Gramp Miller said, "I gotta be goin', too—*some-body's* gotta do some work around the place."

Turning to leave, Tony stopped and snapped his fingers, pointing to Gramp. "Almost forgot. We *may* have to reshoot that cattle scene. Can we talk about setting a time?"

Without looking around, Gramp said, "Okay, I'll be right out."

Tony tapped the foot of Jo's bed and said, "Take care of yourself. Glad it's nothing more serious." Waving at Jo, Pat smiled and said, "Yes, and we'll see you later."

They turned, walked silently out of the room, and neither uttered a word until Tony was holding the Bronco's door open for Pat. "Did that story of hers sound as strange to you as it did to me?"

Pat's head bobbed up and down. "But not as strange as the questions! 'What're you looking for?' 'What're you after?' 'Do you do the same kind of work *he* does?'" She stood by the door and frowned at Tony. "What in the world do you suppose she was talking ab..."

Then they heard Gramp's boots clomp-clomping across the parking lot. They turned and watched his animated, arm-swinging, straight-backed approach.

"Hey!" he yelled out. "Listen!" He started talking when he was still ten feet away and didn't give them a chance to get a word in. "Pay no mind to what that little girl says." Now he stood between them, squinting up at Tony, then at Pat, back and forth, his crinkled gray eyes nervous and worried. "Listen. Jo's

got so much goin' on in her mind right now—" He
stopped, glanced at Pat, and spit out the worst swear
word that he ever used in front of a lady. "Shoot! A
person worries like that, she's *bound* to come out with
screwball ideas. Best thing to do is, just let it slide." He
jammed both fists into his back pockets and looked at
Tony, changing to a new subject. "Okay. You wanted
to talk abut the cattle again?"

"Uh"—Tony stuttered a little, sorting through all
the questions he wanted to ask about Jo, till he remembered his question about the cattle—"Right.
We'll recheck and retime the footage we shot yesterday, before the stampede, to make sure that we have
enough. But, if we find that we didn't get enough, is
it possible to use the cattle again on Tuesday?"

"Yup." He looked at Tony, at Pat, and back at
Tony. "That's it?"

Tony smiled and shrugged. "Yup."

"Actually, no," Pat said. Surprised, they both
looked at her and before anybody else could say anything she hurried on. "Jo said, 'Last year JayDee
showed up again.'" Gramp scowled but she didn't
stop. "Did he go away? Where'd he been before he
'showed up again'?"

Gramp turned his head slowly and his narrowed
eyes scanned the front of the cream-colored hospital
and up to the clear morning sky. "Well," he said finally, still looking away, "I s'pose you'd just ask
somebody else, anyway. He was in jail."

Tony's eyebrows shot up and Pat blurted the words right back at Gramp. "He was in jail?"

When he answered, the sound in his voice was like the look in his eyes, nervous and sad. "Not jail, really. Prison."

He turned and his boots grated on the asphalt as he stomped away toward his pickup and Pat heard him cuss again. "Shoot!"

TWELVE

Saturday (continued)

THE SHORT FALLS is a north-flowing river. That fact alone is enough to make it unusual.

It's also cold. And it stays cold, even while it's running through country where daytime summer temperatures climb as high as one hundred degrees and more.

The Short Falls River is cold because it comes out of glacier-fed springs high in the Cascade Mountains. From 'way back in the mountains down to Short Falls Lake behind the dam at Conroy—seventy-five miles— every single inch of river is so cold that, when somebody sticks a finger in, he usually lets out a yell and yanks it back. If a person is foolish enough to try that with a bare foot he's a candidate for cardiac arrest.

A trout fisherman working the upper Short Falls one spring morning took a break for coffee. The river was so cold that his waders wouldn't go back in.

The Short Falls is unusual for other reasons.

For the rest of its course, from Conroy to the Columbia River ninety-eight miles north, the Short Falls is one of America's most used and most dangerous rivers.

Crossing the Central Oregon plateau it reaches a rate of flow just over four miles per hour, comparable to the much more famous Colorado. It cuts through coulees so deep they sometimes rival the Grand Canyon. Here and there along the way where the coulee walls or the banks narrow, it shoots through the funnel as fast as twenty miles an hour or more.

And the Short Falls River is alive with startling contrasts.

Families on picnics, campers, backpackers, and rafters use the summertime river for recreation, to renew themselves and rest. Scattered along its banks they find shelter from the baking sun under swaying canopies of willow trees or Spanish olives, or in the long shadows thrown by stands of stately Lombardy poplars.

But they also learn, very quickly, to watch for deadly water hemlock, scorpions, and rattlesnakes.

Through serene and lovely passes, the glittering sun-touched ripples invite canoers to come and drift in lazy meanders. As it tumbles the smooth round stones and pumice pebbles along a sandy shore, the river seems to chuckle. Brushing against a shaded canyon wall, it seems to whisper.

But the chuckle could be the start of a backwater that will grow into a boat-spinning eddy. And the whisper from the canyon wall might be the sudden, unnoticed rush of current that builds on the outside of a river's bend.

Currents in a curve like that can overpower any boat, any oarsman, and mash them against the canyon wall or drive them through the curve, out of control, into murderous white-water rapids.

The Short Falls has thirty-four rapids. Some are comparatively short and calm with a few white-topped riffles and little standing waves. River-rafting guides rate these rapids as Class One or Class Two. The classification goes up as the danger goes up. The highest is Class Six. In Class Six rapids, people get killed.

The Short Falls River has several Sixes. One of the roughest is nineteen miles downstream from Conroy, where the river's elevation drops thirty feet in three hundred and fifty yards. Locals call the place Crazy Man Rapids. They say they call it Crazy Man because "if you try to take a boat through there—hardboat *or* inflatable—you're nuts."

Crazy Man has standing waves twenty feet high. There's a suckhole near the right bank that once swallowed an eighteen foot inflatable raft with six people aboard. Fifty yards downriver, two people came up. One lived. The boat and the rest of the people are still missing.

However, the site that Tony had picked for shooting the rafting sequence was well away from any such hazards. It was a placid piece of river about a half-mile below the dam. He and Director Nobu Okumura had agreed that, by placing the camera on shore at about water level and shooting over the few riffles and short, standing waves off-shore, they'd give the scene plenty of flavor.

And by keeping the action upriver, there'd be no chance for the raft they were shooting to get into the rough water downriver—Dead Mary Rapids, about three-quarters of a mile below the camera site. A little way below Dead Mary was the falls that gave the Short Falls River its name, but the crew was in no danger of getting near either one.

The camera setup was on a rock outcropping along the river's east bank. The outcropping was actually a wide, flat shelf of basalt running down in an easy slope from the narrow asphalt access road right into the river—a natural launching ramp. Over the years, so many people had used it to put their boats in the water that the rough gray basalt was worn as smooth as a trailer hitch.

Tony and Pat drove onto it just as a white Oregon State Police car drove away. The instant Tony saw the trooper leaving he whacked the Bronco's steering wheel. "Shoot! As Gramp would say."

"Or words to that effect," Pat added. "What's wrong?"

"I don't know. Something's making me nervous. Damn!" He pulled onto the smooth rock ledge and parked beside the camera van.

Climbing down from the Bronco he checked the other vehicles lined up there—van, equipment truck, cast's station wagon, and crew bus—all for the television company. Behind him, parked well away from the television vehicles, sat a beat-up yellow pickup and another van, this one blue with "Conroy Boats—Sales & Rentals" painted on its dented, dusty side.

"The guide's not here," Tony said quietly.

"What guide?"

"A river guide, from Bend. A rafting expert." He looked toward the river. "He's supposed to be here today to take Dennis Shimada and the boy down the river in the raft. But his truck isn't here." He craned his neck around at the van again. "That's JayDee's pickup, but I wonder who belongs to that blue van."

"Wait a minute!" Pat swung around to face him in front of the Bronco, planting one hand on her hip and shading her eyes with the other. "You're not taking that boy *down the river!* Here?"

"No-no-no." He pointed upriver. "He'll be in the raft with Shimada and—what the hell!" He stopped, staring, arm straight out, pointing. "They're already there. And they've got the raft in the water."

About a hundred yards upstream, three crewmen stood on a narrow strip of rocky shoreline at the edge of the river. One man, standing beside a thick coil of bright yellow nylon rope, let a length of the rope dangle loosely through his hands as it ran out to a gray inflatable raft—actually a heavy-gauge plastic tube, sixteen inches in diameter, shaped into a blunt-tipped rectangle around a floor of equally strong plastic.

The fourteen foot raft bobbed lightly on the water, its slightly up-tilted bow and stern dipping toward the water as if eager to get away. The other two men waded in the shallows with their arms hooked over the tube, holding the raft in place.

Dennis Shimada and young Norio Sakata sat side by side on the round, bulbous bow. Across from them, at the stern, sat JayDee Hampton.

Tony's head wagged back and forth. "And what the hell is JayDee doing in that raft!"

"Tono-san!" Nobu shouted, walking up from the water's edge where the camera was mounted on a short tripod.

About thirty feet to the right of the camera, a sunburned young man sat on a large rock in front of a fifteen-foot metal motorboat that was half in, half out of the river. Donna Hughes sat beside him, watching Dennis Shimada in the raft upstream.

Tony turned away from Pat and took a few steps down the ramp toward Nobu hunching his shoulders up to his ears and holding his arms out to the side, asking Nobu in the worldwide pantomime meaning, "What's going on?"

The answer he got was another question. "You did not speak with police officer?"

Gesturing upriver, Tony came back with questions of his own. "How did JayDee get in that raft with Shimada and Norio? Where's the guide?"

"Ah. You did not speak with the officer." Nobu ducked his head in greeting to Pat, who had stayed by the Bronco several feet behind Tony. Now he and Tony stood side by side looking upriver toward the raft. "Guide cannot come."

"Oh, no." Frowning, Tony cocked his head, rubbing one hand across the back of his neck.

Nobu shrugged. *"Shoganii,"* he said.

Tony'd heard the word several times during the past three weeks, when they had to revise dialogue or change a scene. "Well, maybe it *can't* be helped, but the guy promised to be here."

"'Two employees sick. He must take people in boats,' he tell police."

"Police?"

"He telephoned State Police. Asked police to radio message to car in vicinity. Sergeant Kelsey came. Very early."

Tony smiled and said, "Great! I mean, I'm sorry the guide has problems and can't get here, but that's good cooperation from the state."

"Very nice."

"At least we won't be standing around with our thumbs up waiting for a no-show guide."

Nobu seemed not to understand and looked at him, grinning. "Excuse me?"

"I mean, *knowing* that the guide won't be here, we won't stand around and wait for him, wasting time."

He paused, looking at Nobu. "I apologize for my arrangement not being satisfactory—"

The director shrugged again. *"Shoganii."*

"—but now we can go ahead and solve *our* problem." Tony nodded toward the raft. "Or have you solved it already? With the cowboy?"

Nobu raised his left fist in front of his chest and popped the thumb up, counting. "He was here." His index finger flipped up. "He said he wants to help." His middle finger jumped out. "He says he has been on this river many times." His fourth finger uncurled and he grinned again. "And the fact is, all we need is another body in the boat. Non-Japanese."

Tony smiled. "And they're getting along alright? JayDee and Shimada?"

"I think so, yes."

"Leave us pray," Tony muttered. Nobu looked at him, surprised, but before he could say anything Tony turned toward Pat. He held out his hand and she started down the ramp as he asked Nobu, "Who's the kid with the motorboat?"

"Ah. More cooperation, as you would say, by Sergeant Kelsey. From hearing the message sent by the guide, he thought that we might need help or advice about the river. So he brought the young man who works in the boat-selling store, and he brought the boat. It may be useful."

Pat reached Tony's outstretched hand and held it, briefly, standing between the two men while she and

Nobu muttered morning greetings again. Then Nobu's radio crackled, he spoke into it, nodded, and hurried away toward the camera.

Tony looked at Pat. "I've been wondering whether you really want to stay here and watch a raft float past. Would you rather go on back to The Lodge and relax?"

"Oh, no. I want to stay—it's interesting." Smiling, she glanced around at the cameraman sitting on the ground behind the camera mounted on its squat tripod, at the crew moving reflectors into place to focus even more sunlight onto the river, at Nobu talking into his radio. "As I said, I don't often get a chance to watch a movie being made."

"You're sure?"

"Yes. Stop worrying about me. You go ahead and work. And if you're nice, someday *you* can come to my office and watch me read a balance sheet."

"Life on the edge, right?" He pointed toward the camera van. "Remember that you can go over there and watch the monitor, too."

"I won't be in the way?"

He shook his head. "But if people start talking loud and moving fast, jump into the Bronco. Otherwise, just pick a spot and stay there and they'll go around you."

"Sounds like the voice of experience," she said, smiling again and squeezing his arm. "Go." Then, "Oh, you didn't answer my question about Norio.

You're not *really* going to let that boy float down the river in a raft without—''

"No."

"—you know that there're some rough rapids down there? And a waterfall?"

"Yes. But there's a rope tied to the back end of the raft. And there are people holding the other end of that rope."

"Clever devil." She started away and stopped. "Won't I see the rope in the picture?"

"Tell you what. If you see the rope, you get to sleep with me tonight."

"And if I don't see it?"

"I get to sleep with you."

"Clever."

"And put your hat on."

"And kinky."

"Not tonight. Now. I hate sleeping with a lady with a sunburned nose." He kissed her quickly on the nose. "Gotta go."

"Good luck."

He hurried down the ramp just as Nobu raised one hand high and spoke rapidly into his radio. Upstream, the two crewmen in the water shoved the raft away and it nosed slowly out into the river. The current caught it and its up-tilted bow bobbed and began turning downstream.

Dennis Shimada had moved to the stern and Norio was in the bow alone, his shiny black hair and the orange collar of his lifejacket just barely showing above the side of the raft. JayDee sat in the driver's seat—athwart the center, facing forward—manning the two nine-foot sweeps, or oars.

Tony and Nobu stood about two feet behind the camera, watching the boat, watching JayDee start to maneuver the sweeps in the oarlocks.

Facing the bow, his stroke was reversed from the normal rowing stroke. So to get forward momentum, he leaned back a little, pulled the handles back to swing the sweeps forward, out of the water, toward the bow. He let the tips dip in. Then he bent across forward, pushing the oars.

"It's awkward," Tony muttered quietly, seeing the sweeps bouncing clumsily forward across the surface, spraying water toward the bow. Nobu nodded. "He'll probably get the rhythm soon." Nobu nodded again. "Should Norio be up there in the bow by himself?"

"Ah," Nobu nodded again and spoke rapidly into his walkie-talkie.

Tony looked upriver where the raft had been launched. The crewmen holding the safety rope played it out slowly and carefully so that it trailed in the water behind the raft. One of the other men crouched over the coil, unwinding it smoothly, a little at a time. The third man moved away from the group and cupped his hands around his mouth, shouting to the boat.

Sitting on the tube in the stern, Dennis Shimada'a head swiveled around and he looked back to shore, pointing to himself.

With big, broad gestures the crewman nodded, pointed again at Dennis, and then gestured toward the bow of the boat.

Dennis turned, looking at the bow.

JayDee had got the rhythm of the sweeps and moved them smoothly over the water, in, and back. "Now," Tony said, more to himself than to anyone, "if he gets turned sideways, I hope he knows enough to keep that downstream oar out of the river."

Dennis looked back to the man on shore, pointing first to himself, then to the bow of the boat where Norio sat.

Once more, the man nodded broadly and pointed to the bow, then bent his arm and swung it in a wide, sweeping arc around and out to his side and held it there, as if he had his arm around the shoulders of a child.

The raft was now well out from shore. Getting closer to the main current, JayDee used the sweeps alternately to maintain position in the line of intense light focused on the river by the reflectors.

Tony glanced down at the camera. The red light was on and the camera was sending pictures back to the truck.

The cameraman's bony bottom squirmed a little on the rock ramp and he curled his long, thin legs into a new position around the squat tripod, but he held his upper body steady, hunched toward his camera, eyes pressed against the viewfinder. His right hand gripped the panning arm, moving almost imperceptibly, holding the raft in the frame. His left hand hovered behind the lens shade, just over the focus lever.

Shifting his eyes out to the raft, Tony asked Nobu, "Look okay?"

Nobu spoke in Japanese to the cameraman and the answer came back in a grunt.

"Good," Nobu said. "But I'm thinking, perhaps if I cut and—"

Another grunt came back, louder, and Tony looked down again. The cameraman's left hand rose up and waggled "no." The camera's red light stayed on.

The raft was still only about twenty yards off-shore, in fairly shallow water but angling toward the middle of the river. Dennis Shimada had slid down off the tube into a kneeling position, apparently trying to figure out the best way to get himself from the back to the front of the raft across its flexible plastic floor. Moving over the slick neoprene was tricky, like being on a floating trampoline.

Shimada started forward. Lifting one knee, he shifted all of his weight to the other, which pushed it harder against the flexing plastic. Under his knee, the bottom of the raft bulged down into the river and he felt the water bumping against it. As he moved, the boat crossed onto a few harmless-looking riffles, an isolated line of small whitecaps made as the water ran across the tops of rocks poking up from the riverbottom. With one arm resting on the side of the raft, Shimada moved over and as his knee pushed into the floor again the boat passed over a rock and cracked it so hard that it knocked his leg back and dropped him facedown on the bottom of the boat.

He grabbed his knee, yelling with pain. JayDee, busy with the oars, peeked over his shoulder. All he caught was a glimpse of Shimada curled up on the floor and the men on shore still playing out the yellow line. He went back to trying to keep the bow downriver. He already seemed to be having a little trouble recovering his downstream oar once it got in the water.

In the bow, Norio diligently did as he'd been told. Following the script, he played the part of a boy having a good time, constantly looking around at the scenery and smiling at the sights along the river. And approximately every five seconds he raised his left hand and pretended to point out something new.

In the stern, Shimada draped his arms over the tube and hauled himself to his feet. Limping, leaning on the tube, he began sliding along the left side toward the bow and Norio. First, though, he had to get past JayDee swinging those nine-foot oars.

THIRTEEN

Saturday (continued)

ON THE RAMP, Tony and Nobu heard Shimada yell and they saw him drop out of sight, but they couldn't see the reason why. Tony guessed that he'd just slipped on the raft's wet floor.

By the time they saw the actor getting up, however, they both knew that they'd have to reshoot the scene—the raft, still slightly upriver from the ramp and the camera, was drifting too far from shore for the camera angle to work, and too near the stronger current in the center of the river for safety.

Nobu radioed the shore crew to pull the raft back for a reshoot as Shimada, ignoring the crippling pain in his knee, worked his way forward bit by bit, pushing his hands against the tube and sliding sideways in gimpy little hop-steps. He made it to the center thwart where he stopped behind JayDee. Hampton was bent far forward with his arms stretched out straight and his hands wrapped around the oar handles, getting ready to rear back for his recovery stroke.

At that moment, the yellow line snapped tight. The boat jerked and stopped. Shimada lurched forward just as JayDee's arm pulled back like a piston, driving his elbow into Shimada's belly just above his groin.

Shimada yelled and doubled over. JayDee, caught by surprise, reacted like a man who thought he was being attacked from behind. He dropped his oar handles and jumped up, straddling the seat as the oars floated free and the boat drifted across the current. With the oars loose in the water, the raft swung over the downstream oar and pushed it under water, blade down. Caught in the current but frozen by its oarlock, the blade snapped off.

The upstream oar had drifted straight out to the side and when the boat swung right, the oar swung left. The current grabbed it and pushed the blade around in an arc toward the stern making its handle wobble over the raft in an opposite arc toward the bow.

JayDee, crouching to keep his balance, grabbed the doubled-over Shimada by the hair with his left hand and cocked his right hand.

At the same time, the men on shore started hauling in the tow line. The backward surge reversed the direction of the oar. The surge, combined with the powerful current, forced the blade back through the water. Pivoting in its oarlock, the nine-foot oar reversed its drive.

As JayDee let go with his punch, the long solid ash handle swung through the air like a baseball bat and cracked the back of his skull.

JayDee crumpled against Shimada and they tumbled back across the raft. Locked together they hit the slick wet tube, slid over it, dropped out of the stern, and slammed down on the yellow rope where it was tied to the D-ring. The D-ring's plastic mounting was already stretched taut by the tension on the yellow line and when they hit it, the mounting snapped.

The raft floated free. Slowly changing direction, it started drifting downriver, with Norio, toward Dead Mary Rapids.

It all happened in less than a minute—so fast that Nobu still had his radio up to his mouth and Tony was still thinking about the cameraman motioning "no cut."

Now, for a second, they both stared at Norio alone in the raft. Tony turned and ran toward the motorboat half-in and half-out of the river.

The young man who apparently owned the aluminum boat, was standing with Donna Hughes watching the action on the river. But when he saw Tony and heard him shouting, "Let's go! Let's go!" he jerked his boat's painter loose from the rock where he'd tied it up, pushed his boat backwards into the river, and hopped in.

Tony ran past Donna and splashed into the water after the boat. He shoved the bow again and rolled over it into the boat. "What's your name?" he yelled.

"Charlie!" The young man shouted, clambering toward the stern.

"I'm Tony! Turn this thing on and let's go get that kid!"

The little outboard clattered and rattled and popped into action as Tony pulled the painter in. He coiled the wet rope over one hand while Charlie spun the boat in a tight circle and headed out toward the raft, then he dropped the coil between the two paddles by his feet and twisted his neck around to look for the men in the water upriver.

The crew had waded in up to their armpits and one of them tossed the yellow line like a lasso to Shimada, who seemed to be swimming toward them and towing the unconscious JayDee.

Tony turned back to the raft. Now about fifty yards off, Norio peered at the motorboat over the top of the tube. His shiny little head looked very lonely in the big empty raft. He waved one small hand. Tony waved back and held his fist out in a cheery "thumbs up" signal, hoping it meant the same in Japanese and not something bawdy.

For an instant, his memory flashed back to the story of the American singer in Rio de Janeiro, rehearsing for her first appearance with a Brazilian orchestra: the rehearsal was awful; the orchestra knew it as well as she did; she told her American conductor to take a ten-minute break; wanting to cheer up the musicians and offer encouragement, she smiled at the orchestra and made the familiar American hand signal for "okay"— tips of thumb and middle finger touching in an "O."

The entire orchestra jumped up and stormed off the stage. That's how she learned that the American hand signal for "okay" means "pig's ass" in Brazil.

Tony waved again to Norio, palm out as if erasing anything he might have signaled. Confident that towing the raft in would be no problem, he turned again and looked toward the ramp. Pat had come down from the camera van and was watching with Nobu. When she saw Tony looking at her, she swung her arms out wide to the side and let them flop back against her legs, a gesture that said, "Now what?"

He raised his hand and repeated the "thumbs-up" signal. She waved back with the "okay" sign and for a second he wondered if she'd heard the story about the singer.

The sound from Charlie's motor changed from a high-pitched whine to a low rumble as he throttled back to let the aluminum boat drift gently toward the raft. They were now about a hundred yards below the ramp and a few hundred yards above the rapids. Watching the raft, Tony spoke over his shoulder to Charlie, raising his voice enough to be heard over the sputtering motor. "Get as close to the bow as you can and I'll work us around so we can tie onto the D-ring in front."

"Okay."

"Then I'll hold the painter and we can tow her back to the ramp."

"Got it."

The sputtering stopped and in the sudden silence the sounds of the moving river came alive. "You don't have to kill the motor. This'll only take a second."

"I didn't kill it. It just died."

The motorboat thumped softly against the side of the raft. Tony's hand rasped on the top of the tube as he grabbed it. Standing in the motorboat he walked his hands along the tube, maneuvering toward the front of the raft. He worked his way past Norio who was squatting in the raft with his hands on the tube. Tony smiled into Norio's worried eyes, patting his hand and ruffling his hair. Then he looked at Charlie. "What do you mean, 'it just died'?"

Charlie screwed the filler cap back on after checking the fuel. "It just died."

"Well, crank it up and let's get out of here. We're not standing still, you know."

Charlie yanked the starter cord. "You're not givin' me any late news." Nothing happened. He kept pulling the cord, answering between grunts. "I live here."

With the boat tucked into the raft's up-tilted bow, they slid down the river. Tony studied the passing cliff-face on the west side. "How fast, do you think?"

"The river? I hear she's been running about three, maybe four miles an hour."

"For a river, I'd guess that's pretty fast."

"Yep."

Charlie rested for a minute. In the sudden quiet, the far away rumble of Dead Mary Rapids was more a feeling than a sound, like sensing distant thunder.

Norio gazed at Tony with a frown on his face and a nervous look in his bright brown eyes. Tony tapped the tube a couple of times, shook his head, and smiled an encouraging, not-to-worry smile. He started another thumbs-up signal but changed his mind. Then they heard the motor catch and he and Norio grinned at each other.

Charlie revved the motor in neutral for a few seconds and throttled back. Tony stooped and picked up the loose end of the painter, ready to thread it through the D-ring to tow the raft. The motor died again. Charlie swore and started yanking the cord.

Tony looked at the rock walls now beginning to rise above both sides of the river. "We waited too long," he said, "trying to get the motor started. If we'd rowed to shore in the first few minutes, we could've hauled out with no trouble."

Silently, Charlie pulled the cord. Tony squinted upriver to where the low east bank had changed into a sheer rock face and started climbing.

"But now that rock wall on the east side'll keep us in the water till it drops down on the other side of the rapids."

Charlie kept working on the motor without saying anything while Tony surveyed the flowing river. "Four miles an hour means one mile in fifteen minutes," he said. "My guess is that we've been out here about five minutes." The motor sputtered but didn't catch. "My next guess is that we've got about four minutes till we hit the rapids."

"I'll get her before that."

"Good. But if you don't—"

"I'll get her."

"—I'd rather take the boy through in the raft than in a hard boat. How 'bout you?"

"I'll stick. And I'll get 'er."

Tony nodded. "Okay if I take one of your paddles?"

"Sure." Charlie shook his head and slumped beside the motor, winded. Tony let the nose of the raft slip past a few feet till the boat and raft were side by side again. He handed a paddle to Norio and rolled himself over the tube and into the raft, dragging the painter behind him.

In the raft, he held the boat close and turned back to Charlie, who sat up and started trying the motor again. "Sparks okay?"

"Sparks okay. Fuel's okay. Everything's okay except the friggin' thing won't start."

"Don't give up."

"Not me."

Now they heard the rapids clearly over the rattle and sputter of the motor.

Tony asked Charlie, "Have you been through Dead Mary?"

"Once. It's not too bad."

"I've just seen it from the road."

Charlie sat back with the cord in his hand. "The first thing is Mary's Hole. Take it on the right and get back in the middle real fast. After that," he shrugged, "all you can do is ride."

"What about a take-out spot?"

"Comin' out of the rapids. That rock face drops down and a little ledge comes in from the right. Don't miss it. The next take-out's on the other side of the falls."

Their voices had gradually got louder to be heard over the roar coming from downriver. Tony's voice was a little higher, too. "You as nervous as I am?"

"Nah. It's not my boat." He went back to yanking the cord. "Besides, I don't have the kid with me."

"Right. Well, listen. I don't think we oughta try to get through together, so I'm gonna shove off from you and wish you luck."

"Same to you."

"Unless you want to ride with us."

"Nah. I'll keep tryin' this sucker."

Tony coiled the painter again, leaned out of the raft, and dropped the coil back into the motorboat. Then, with a little push on its bow, he separated the bow from the raft.

The distance between the two increased quickly as the heavier, bigger raft moved downstream. He turned to look downriver and instead looked straight into the big brown eyes of Norio, who was sitting by his shoulder.

Tony grinned, pointed to the river ahead, and made a roller coaster motion with his hand. He turned Norio around and sat him on the thwart facing forward, then sat behind him on the right hand tube.

The river seemed to pick up speed and focus itself on a V-shaped slick that narrowed between two big boulders in the middle of the river.

As he studied the river ahead, Tony picked up the paddle and shifted to the left side of the raft. Under the roar coming from the river he heard another noise behind him. He looked back at the boat. Charlie was sitting and waving his arm behind a little cloud of bright blue smoke. He had the motor running but it was too late to come and get the raft.

And upriver, far behind Charlie, the crew was wading through the water carrying a limp body.

Tony turned around just as the raft hit the slick and went gliding down the narrowing V between the two boulders. He grabbed Norio as they sailed off the lip of a three-foot fall and smacked down in a swirl of creamy green water.

Fighting toward the right side of the river, he dug his paddle frantically into whipping, churning water that tried to push the raft left. At the edge of the froth he slipped into a patch of smooth water on the right side of a squat gray rock dripping with wet moss. Taking a breath, he glanced around the rock.

On the other side, flooding water curled back on itself and fell in green sheets over the huge, prostrate trunk of a dead cedar jammed crosswise between two more boulders. Racing along the trunk the river piled up on itself again, climbed the back of another boulder, then poured over the top and crashed down into a watery green hole. Twenty feet downstream a granite ledge cut into the river, blocked the rushing torrent, and forced it to circle back in a foaming, frightening, thundering whirlpool. Mary's Hole.

Tony caught Norio looking at the whirlpool. The boy's head swiveled on his neck like an owl's, seeing everything. His mouth pursed into a tight O, his eyes glittered, and he flattened his hands over his ears to keep out the roar.

After paddling across a slow eddy to the right side of the river, Tony turned the raft and drifted downstream. He moved back on the tube to sit near the stern, holding the paddle in the water like a rudder. He used it for a stroke every once in a while, but mostly he floated and watched the river ahead. Behind, the noise from Mary's Hole quieted quickly. Ahead, Dead Mary Rapids waited around the gentle bend to the left.

He paddled through the slack water at the curve. Across the river, swift water raced around the outside of the bend. Dark streaks of water smeared the rusty canyon walls and spume flew through the air.

Around the curve, twenty yards downriver, a row of underwater rocks made a thin, rippling white line across the water to mid-river. The line stopped at a granite rock thirty feet tall and twenty feet wide. Past the rock, the left side of the river rolled so hard over the rocky bottom that the surface looked like whipped cream with peaks five feet tall. "Stay on the right side," Charlie had said.

Beyond the white line, the right side became gradually rougher—the ripples became whitecaps which became waves which became haystacks, tall white piles of standing water like ocean surf.

Tony tapped the tube to get Norio's attention, then grinned and dipped his hand through the air in another roller coaster motion. "Some encouragement, hey, kid?" he said. Norio looked at him and turned away.

By now they'd crossed over the white line and the river began to get louder again. It wasn't the beginning of a thunderous roar—not the kind of sound that came from Mary's Hole. It was more of a liquid, sizzling sound, as when bacon begins to fry.

The raft seemed to move faster. It began to tremble. It dipped into a trough and came up in the whitecaps. Into another trough and water poured into the bow. Norio looked around. Tony grinned and nodded. Norio turned away again. They hit another trough and the raft was slow coming up. A wall of water pounced over the tube and doused both of them. Norio's head jerked around and he was truly alarmed but all Tony could do was keep paddling, grin, and yell. Norio hunkered down.

The raft rippled and bounced on the waves and Tony paddled as hard as he could to keep the raft bow-on to the rapids and on the right side of the river, because the left side was rougher.

Water pounded the raft and streamed in from all sides. The raft bucked and twisted and skewed across, over, and sometimes into the river. Sometimes Tony's paddle hit the river and sometimes it crunched on rock and sometimes it just waved through foam. The boat tunneled into troughs and bounced off boulders and by this time Norio was yelling as loud as Tony. They yelled and screamed and laughed and couldn't hear themselves half the time because the river noise swallowed everything they did.

They felt the river whacking the raft from every angle, pushing, pulling, twisting, thumping, all at the same time. They tossed up and crashed down and plowed through flashing white water in a continuous, liquid, rolling rumble of noise that suddenly stopped. They shot through the last wave and were done.

Astonished, they looked around at where they'd been and barely heard a sound. The man and the boy looked at each other, dripping wet. Then they pointed at each other and grinned.

Just ahead, on another shelf running into the river, Pat and Nobu waited by the camera van with a few of the crew. Tony steered the raft in. Nobu and a couple of the men hauled the bow a little way out of the river while Norio chattered rapidly.

"What's he saying?" Tony asked Nobu.

"He wants to do it again."

FOURTEEN

Saturday (continued)

TONY STRADDLED the raft tube, resting. Nobu hoisted Norio over the tube and took him away to get dry and changed.

Pat came down to the river's edge. She stood beside Tony, paying no attention to the water lapping at her white Nikes. With one hand on the raft and the other on the knee of his soaked khakis, she boosted herself up on the raft to sit between his legs. She slapped his wet knee and said, "Well. Lookin' a little soggy there, Captain Ahab."

She threw her arms around his neck and he dropped his paddle into the water in the bottom of the raft where it splashed and sloshed around as he hugged her. She breathed a deep sigh into his ear. "I don't know what we're gonna do with you. One day it's 'Gunsmoke' and the next day it's *Moby Dick*."

She pushed herself away a little. "If we hadn't rafted some of these rivers ourselves, I'd've been really worried about you." Craning her neck back, she asked, "But why did you do that?"

"*Somebody* had to go after the kid."

"There was an entire TV crew—"

"Nobody closer."

"Nobu? The cameraman?"

"Maybe I thought of it first. Anyway—" He shrugged, as if to change the subject.

Pat massaged the tops of his shoulders through his wet shirt before she sat back. "You're soaked. That water must be freezing. I hope you don't catch cold."

Tony started pulling off his wet sneakers and socks. He gestured at the damp front of her tan safari shirt. "You, too."

She looked down at the damp impression on her breasts. "That'll teach me to hug river rats." She shook her head. With the tips of her thumbs and forefingers she lifted the damp shirt, flapping it.

He poked a finger between the buttons and ran the nail across her skin. "We could take our clothes off and let them dry on a rock," he said.

"I'm afraid that would be deadly for tourism in Central Oregon." She jumped off the raft. "*And* Japanese-American relations."

"Speaking of which," Tony said, sliding off beside her, "let's go sit in the sun and dry off while you tell me what happened with JayDee and Shimada."

As Pat told it, Shimada and the crew hauled JayDee out of the water and carried him, still unconscious, back to the rock ledge where the camera was set up.

He lay stretched out in the center of a spreading dark, damp stain a few feet above the camera tripod.

Water ran out of his blonde hair and his clothes and his socks—he'd left his boots in his truck. And when he sat up coughing and shaking his head, more water sprayed out of his hair and the drops freckled the rock and the shoes of the people standing around him.

Pat and several of the crew had come down from the truck, but when JayDee looked up and scanned the faces looking back, he stopped at Dennis Shimada. Glaring and growling he said "You hit me from behind, you sneaky son-of-a-bitch" and rolled over to push himself up.

One of the Japanese bent and grabbed his arm to help but JayDee jerked away. "Get your hands off, you—"

"No one attacked you," Shimada said loudly. "No one hit you."

Pat spoke up. She nodded her head and said, "That's right, nobody hit you. It was the oar—"

"Bull shit."

"—it was loose in the water and the handle came around and hit your head."

"Bull shit."

Most of the Japanese didn't understand the words, but standing there in a loose circle around Pat and JayDee they understood the sounds and the feeling in the air. They glanced at each other, shuffling and shifting their feet.

Pat took a breath before she threw her next words at Hampton. "Listen to me! You're old enough to control that temper of yours, young man, and if you swear at me again I'll take you over my knee and—"

"Bull shit, lady, and that goes for that narc husba—"

She slapped him so hard that his head spun and water sprayed out of his hair and speckled her face.

Before JayDee got his balance Nobu stepped in and grabbed his arm and started him moving up the ramp toward his truck. "Enough, Mr. Hampton! Go, please!"

JayDee shook him off but before he could say anything Nobu stepped up and stood nose-to-nose with him. Nobu's voice was quiet but tight and harsh. His whole body quivered with rage. "Go. You tried to help today and thank you but bad things happened. Bad things *always* happen when you come here. Stay away from this production. Go. Do not come back."

The rest of his crew ranged around Nobu in an arc, flanking JayDee. Everything was quiet, except for the river sound. Then, from downstream, came the putter of a motorboat starting.

JayDee took a step backwards and his wet socks left dark runny footprints on the rock ledge. He studied the tense and furious Nobu standing in front of him. He flexed his jaw and scraped his knuckles across a thin trickle of blood on the corner of his mouth.

"Okay," he said. He glanced at the blood smear on the back of his hand and shot a look at Pat. "Okay for right now. But me and a few friends may come around and show you and your fink husband and your little black-haired friends here who belongs in this country and who don't.''

He turned and walked up the slope toward his truck, but Pat didn't notice the wet footprints he left behind. Instead, she stared at the back of JayDee's wide, wet leather belt. It glittered in the sunlight. The glitter came from steel studs set in the back of his belt, spelling out his name—studs that looked exactly like the one she and Tony had found in the hall after someone dumped the rattlesnakes in their room. And there was a stud missing from the crossbar in the last letter in JAYDEE.

Listening to Pat describe what she saw and heard—and did—while he was riding the rapids, Tony stretched out on his stomach on the warm rock ledge. He listened and at the same time tried to point the seat of his wet pants at the sun; the knit shirt he'd spread beside him was already nearly dry.

Pat sat beside him under the shade of her wide-brimmed planter's hat, her hands clasped around her drawn-up knees.

When she told him about JayDee's studded belt he rolled over on his back and pushed himself up on his elbows, squinting at Pat. "You're sure?"

"Sure of what? That the studs were similar? Positive. That one was missing from his belt? Positive. And do I think the missing stud is the one we found? I'm sure enough to give it to your state trooper friend—or any other policeman we see." She squirmed a little, stretching her legs out in front of her on the rock ledge.

"Fine." Tony sat up and stared out toward the sparkling river, now running smooth, gentle, and deceptive between the rapids and the falls. "But, assume that JayDee is the one who put the rattlesnakes in that room—" Pat shivered. Tony nodded. "Right— but *if* he put them in there, why did he do it? Because he thought it was Shimada's room? Would he try to *kill* Shimada just because he might be making it with Jo? That seems pretty weird."

"He's a pretty weird guy."

"Okay, so he's a punk as far as we're concerned."

"He's a pain in the tail."

"Sure. To us, maybe." Tony held up a hand. "But remember what Jo said. In some way, for some reason, JayDee apparently did something that made a change in that family. Something that Jo thought was good. At least, for awhile." He dropped his hand to her knee.

"Fine. But my interest is *this* family and I do not see contact with that punk as being a major benefit." She laid her hand on top of his. "I want to digress for a minute."

"All right."

"I've noticed that Central Oregon rocks are very hard."

"Yes. I'll help you up."

They stood and Pat jiggled in place for a couple of seconds while Tony pulled on his nearly dry shirt and stuffed his feet back into his still-wet socks and sneakers.

Pat said, "Getting back to JayDee, I've been thinking about what William Edmonds said—at breakfast?—about you switching rooms with Shimada. What if JayDee knew that you'd already done it?"

Tony's mouth turned down for a moment. "That would mean that he meant the snakes for me." He shook his head. "Why?"

Pat shrugged. "He's a punk."

He shrugged back at her. "Even a punk has a reason for doing something. Not a good one, maybe, but it sounds okay to the punk." He put his arm around her shoulders and they started toward the camera van. "Now let *me* digress. I have a proposition for you."

"Aha!"

"Steady. I propose that we get the car and go look for a restaurant and—" Tony stopped, frowning at Pat. "Wait a second. JayDee said something just before you slugged him."

"Slapped."

"Okay, slapped."

"He said, and I quote, 'Bull shit, lady.'"

"After that," Tony prompted. "He said something after that." Trying to recall more of Pat's story, he murmured "—'and that goes for'—"

"Good Lord. 'And that goes for your narc husband, too.' That's what he started to say and I was so mad it didn't really register. Good Lord."

"He thinks I'm a cop? What have I done that makes him think I'm a cop?" Tony shook his head. "And a narc, at that. Hard to believe." He paused, and the corners of his mouth turned down. "Makes you wonder about JayDee Hampton, though. If he thinks I'm a cop, why does he put snakes in my room? To shake me up? Try to scare me off?" Now he raised his eyebrows. "Scare me off *what*? Is JayDee doing drugs? And am I supposed to know about it?" Then he grinned and said, "See? What did I tell you: Even punks have reasons."

They walked on up the ledge, crowded into the camera van—Norio, now dry, sat next to Tony for the first time in their acquaintance—and rode back to the Bronco. Then Tony and Pat switched cars and drove toward Conroy looking for a place to have a late lunch.

"From the way that little boy snuggled up to you, I think you've found a new friend."

Tony smiled. "Comrades in arms, now, after battling the rapids together."

Pat's gaze turned out across the fields toward the mountains. When she turned back to Tony her eyes were misty. "Bring back memories? Having a little form tucked against your side again?"

He glanced over, smiling. "Jenny and Dan?" He reached out and their fingers touched and curled together on the seat between them. "Been a long time since our kids have done any snuggling, hasn't it? At least, with *us*." Pat nodded. "Miss it?"

"Sometimes." She nodded again and looked away. "Sometimes I really do," she said out the window.

"Me, too." He put both hands back on the wheel. "I will admit I'm not sorry that that period is behind us, but sometimes I miss the kids being kids. Having 'college men and women' around the house is just not the same."

"And it won't be long before the 'college man and woman' are gone, too."

They rode together in silence. Tony watched the road. Pat looked at the fields. And somehow during those few minutes, without knowing it, they were holding hands again.

Men and machines were working in the nearest fields, harvesting mint, and the wind blowing in carried its peculiar, dusty scent.

"Well." Pat cleared her throat. "I didn't mean to get carried away, there." Tony's hand patted hers. "What I wanted to ask was, did you really get enough footage of the boy in the raft this morning? It seemed to me that everything went to pieces after just a few minutes.''

''Nobu said the actual tape time ran almost sixty seconds, and—''

''Less than a minute?''

Tony's head wagged up and down. ''—and almost thirty seconds of that is useable, so—''

''Less than *half* a minute?''

''—so with the intercuts they'll have a good long sequence of Norio on the river. Later today they'll shoot him and Shimada getting *out* of the raft on that ramp where we parked. So, when the picture's all put together, it'll look as though they made a nice little trip downriver.''

''Wait a second. 'Intercuts'?''

''Right. Remember how, in the raft, he kept pointing at things? He'd ride and point at something and ride and point again? Every five seconds or so.''

''Yes. Looked a little strange.''

''But when they put it all together to make the movie, they'll insert, every time he points, a shot of what he's looking at.'' As Tony explained the sequence, he emphasized the word *cut* with a loud finger snap. ''Norio points to the side, *cut:* There's a deer, drinking out of the river. He points up, *cut:* An osprey swoops down over the water and snatches a fish. He points ahead, *cut:*—'' He stopped and flipped his hand out, palm up. ''And so on. Those are intercuts.''

Pat was silent, studying his profile. "Where did they get all those deer and ospreys? And so ons."

"They've been shooting birds and animals and scenery ever since they arrived from Japan. That cameraman is terrific. He's picked up shots of bears, badgers, eagles, deer, just about anything you can think of. Every day he spots something new. They'll just pick some and drop them in."

"Sounds like cheating." Pat turned and looked out her window.

Tony shook his head. "Artistic license."

They reached the northern outskirts of Conroy and passed a big blue billboard announcing the approach of "Conroy Industrial Park," a sparse cluster of dusty buildings on the right. The biggest building was a chunky, gray grain elevator with Purina's red-and-white checkerboard logo on its stack. Somewhere behind it, a processing plant still exhaled the heavy, too-sweet stink of cooking mint and the odor—so unlike its fresh-cut scent—blew through Pat's open window.

She turned back to Tony and saw him squirming on his seat. "What's wrong?"

"Shorts didn't get dry. Itchy."

"Serves you right. 'Artistic license' my foot."

"I'm glad you agree."

Tony flipped the turn signal and let the Bronco begin to slow. Two hundred yards past the industrial park stood a sign with a line of flashing pink light-bulbs dancing around a pink drawing of an apron with the words "Granny's—Good Eats" written across it in script. The restaurant was a large one-story frame building painted periwinkle blue. He turned into the red-gravel driveway and parked beside a big white sedan. It had red-and-blue lights across the top and "Oregon State Police" lettered in black on its side.

Walking into the restaurant, Tony said, "Do you suppose we could be lucky enough to run into Kelsey in here?" And there at the counter sat Sergeant Kelsey, sliding his fork under a mouthful of boysenberry pie *a la mode*.

After they ordered, Kelsey brought his coffee cup over and slid into their booth beside Tony. "Everything go all right on the river?"

Pat sipped from her glass of ice water as Tony said, "Fine." She almost choked.

"Well," he drawled, "there were a couple of problems."

Together they described the morning's events, ending with Pat giving an edited version of her confrontation with JayDee Hampton.

"So what you're telling me is: JayDee Hampton has a studded belt. You think that one of the studs is missing. You found a stud outside your room after you found the snakes *inside*. If the stud came from Hampton's belt, he may have put the snakes there. Is that what you're saying?"

Tony and Pat nodded.

"So one thing we'll have to do is check the stud. Where is it?"

Simultaneously, Pat said, "I gave it to William Edmonds" and Tony said, "I gave it to Pat."

Kelsey said, "Okay. Let's find it. Soon. Now, another thing you're telling me is that *if* Hampton put the snakes in your room it *may* be because he thinks you're a cop."

Tony nodded. "That's what he said."

"Strange."

Pat said, "A narcotics cop, at that."

Tony leaned against the back of the booth, looking at Pat. "I just remembered something else. In the hospital, talking to Jo Miller: She said to me, 'What are you after? What're you looking for?'"

Pat's head went slowly up and down. "Something like that. That's right."

Kelsey said, "*She* thinks you're a cop, too?"

"Sounds like it, doesn't it?" Tony leaned forward again, elbows on the table. "Now. This is what I really wanted to ask you. Let's say that JayDee thinks I'm a cop. And let's say that Jo Miller thinks so, too, because maybe she got the idea from JayDee. My question is, why should they care?—what're they doing that makes them so worried about a narcotics cop?"

Before Kelsey could answer, a short round waitress brought two bacon-lettuce-and-tomato sandwiches and two glasses of iced tea for Pat and Tony. She put the bill beside Tony's plate and said, "A pleasant repast."

The waitress walked away and Pat glanced at Tony and shrugged. "Beats 'Enjoy.'"

Without turning his head, Sergeant Kelsey looked at Pat, at Tony, and back to Pat. After a long silence he said, "As I mentioned to you once before, Mr. Pratt, police in rural areas have the same problems as police in the cities. The same things happen here that happen in Portland and Seattle and San Franciso and wherever. Including drugs. We, and several other law enforcement agencies, have investigations under way in this area."

"Is JayDee under investigation for dealing drugs?"

Kelsey let another few seconds go by. "It's one thing he was suspected of in Portland."

"Are you saying that he's under suspicion—under surveillance—now?"

"What I said was, he was suspected of it in Portland. What you heard is up to you. And I can't change it."

Sergeant Kelsey flipped up the flap on his shirt pocket and took out his sunglasses and his hard gray eyes disappeared behind the dark green lenses. His face turned to Pat and in a quiet, pleasant tone he said, "Nice seeing you again, Mrs. Pratt." His face turned to Tony and his voice was quiet and pleasant but with a hard edge. "You're a writer, so maybe you have a very good nose for a story. Otherwise, picking Win

Miller's place for part of this movie was a really odd coincidence."

He was going through the front door before Tony and Pat stopped staring after him. Then Pat shoved the remaining half of her sandwich aside. "That's the kind of comment that makes me forget about eating. Or maybe that's the kind of sandwich that makes me forget about eating."

"Mysterious," Tony said, and bit down on a pickle slice.

"Kelsey's comment or the sandwich?"

"Kelsey's comment." He reached over and picked a slice of pickle off her plate. "Don't you want this?" He flipped it into his mouth and chewed on it as he reached for money to pay the bill. "That remark of his takes a little chewing on, too."

They were driving away when Pat tapped her sternum and asked, "Who was the writer who said to stay away from restaurants called 'Mom's'?"

"'Never play cards with a man named Doc and never eat at a place called 'Mom's'—something like that? I think it was Steinbeck."

"What if the place is called 'Granny's'? Does that mean it's twice as bad?"

They drove south, talking sporadically, taking apart Sergeant Kelsey's closing remark. They went through Conroy and on down Highway 97 toward the turnoff to the Short Falls Reservation and The Lodge. Approaching the intersection just beyond the Indian Gift

Shop and Information Center, Tony slowed for the right turn under the flashing yellow light.

Straightening out of the turn, a movement caught his eye and he glanced into the parking lot. In the shade of three willow trees, way in the back, JayDee's raunchy yellow pickup was again parked by the same shiny new red Cadillac convertible, driver's side to driver's side. The slick-haired man in the convertible reached toward the pickup and JayDee snatched something out of his hand and drove away.

FIFTEEN

Sunday

PAT ARGUED with Tony that his "contribution to international amity on Saturday had been above and beyond," as she put it; that the TV production could get along without him on Sunday; that he'd earned a day of rest.

So while the cast and crew answered their usual early call, Tony and Pat slept. Emerging from sleep they found themselves in the middle of a long, slow waking-up exercise. Afterwards, they gave themselves another treat—breakfast by room service and all morning with the Sunday papers, including one crossword puzzle apiece.

In the early afternoon they drove into Conroy again to visit Jo Miller at the hospital. "I think we should go," Pat said in the car, "but I can't explain why. Just a feeling."

She'd turned to sit sideways on the seat, left knee bent and pointing at Tony, left ankle tucked under right leg, left arm stretching along the top of the seat toward his shoulder. "I think that whatever problems she has are getting to be more than she can handle. Maybe talking to someone from 'outside' will help.

Another woman. An older woman, maybe. And," she added with a wry smile, leaning across and patting him on the thigh, "we must remember I'm old enough to be her mother."

"You? Nonsense!" Tony glanced at his wife, smiling, before he turned back to the road. "Anyway, don't forget—Jo may want to talk to a 'mother figure' and you may be it, but she also thinks you're married to a cop."

Pat was quiet for a while. Finally, she made a little clicking noise with the corner of her mouth and said, "Yes. Well, I hope I can work my way through that."

At the hospital it was slow going with Jo. Maybe her sore ribs bothered her more than they had the day before. Or maybe it was something else. Whatever it was it had turned her tan face pale. Dark circles puffed under her eyes. Worry lines pinched between her brows.

Gramp stood beside her bed but even he hadn't been able to pull her out of her grim mood.

And Donna Hughes hadn't helped. Tony and Pat heard about her almost as soon as they walked into Jo's room.

They'd barely said hello when Gramp grinned and yipped out, "That interpreter or whatever you call it, she come through here"—he laughed a couple of high-pitched croaks—"she come through here like she was a private eye or somethin'," he said. Still groaning, he looked at Tony, "Or maybe I shouldn't say such a thing in front of you."

"Such a thing as what, 'private eye'?" Tony grinned back at him.

But Jo was grim. "Yes. Don't real cops hate private detectives?"

"I don't know." Tony shrugged. "I'm not a cop."

Smiling, Gramp said, "Sure you're not," and winked.

Pat stepped in. "But he's not!"

"Right," Gramp said. "Anyway, that Donna come in here and—"

Jo butted in, sneering. "Came in here as if she cared about *me*. She doesn't care about *me*. She hates me. Because of Dennis. All she *really* wanted to know is where JayDee was."

"JayDee?" Pat asked Jo. "Why does she want to see JayDee?"

Gramp chuckled. "That's a real high-strung lady. Prob'ly wants to clean JayDee's clock 'cause he stuck his elbow in her Jap playmate. Maybe bent her toy."

"Gramp!" Jo said.

Tony glanced at Pat and then at Gramp. "I'll never understand how gossip gets around so fast. How did you hear about *that*?"

"Charlie. The kid from the boat store. Stops in a bar after you and him kept the little kid from cloggin' up the rapids. Has a beer. Tells the story. Next thing you know it's all over the county."

Tony shook his head. "It *is* like jungle drums."

There was a pause till Pat said, "Well. Did Donna find JayDee?"

"No!" Jo answered Pat, but her eyes were on Gramp. "I mean, I'm not sure."

Gramp returned her look. "No. Like I told her, JayDee's out at the ranch. Workin' with Win."

Pat caught Tony's eye and glanced quickly at Gramp, then toward the door.

"Listen, Gramp," he said, "I want to talk to you about reshooting that scene with some of your cattle."

Frowning, Gramp turned his head toward Tony. "I thought we settled that."

"Yeah, but I have a couple of questions. Maybe we could talk about it outside—get some air, and save Jo and Pat from hearing a lot of dull details."

In quick succession Gramp studied Pat's face, Jo's, and Pat's again before he said, "Oh. Okay." Passing the little humps in the sheet made by Jo's feet, he wrapped a hand around one, wiggled it, and without looking at her said, "Stick around," and walked out the door with Tony.

Pat moved slowly from the foot of the bed to Jo's side as she said, "I don't want to intrude, but there are two things I'd like to say to you. One is, my husband is *not* a policeman." She raised her hand to stop Jo from interrupting. "He wouldn't be, couldn't be, and shouldn't be a cop. Of *any* kind."

"But JayDee said—"

Shaking her head, Pat said, "He's a writer. And sometimes, as you can see, he also works in television."

"JayDee says that's just a cover."

Pat shook her head again. "I promise."

"But he's so *sure*."

"JayDee's wrong. About a lot of things. But we can talk about that in a minute." Standing beside the bed Pat began fussing gently with the sheet, straightening, smoothing, tucking.

"The other thing I'd like to say is this: Something other than those sore ribs is bothering you. You know how a person can feel these things sometimes?" Without saying a word Jo sat up, Pat plumped and rearranged her pillows, and Jo sat back again. "As I said, I don't want to intrude, but please tell me if there's anything I can do to help. Even if it's just to sit here and listen."

Again, without a word, Jo scooted over a little and Pat cocked a hip and perched on the side of the bed. Reaching for the carafe and glass on the bedside table she said, "How 'bout some fresh water?"

TONY AND GRAMP walked outside. The old man stopped under the shading portico at the little hospital's main entrance. Tony kept walking.

After taking several steps across the parking lot, Tony, without looking back, swung his arm around motioning for Gramp, and the old man scuttled after him with his Fred Flintstone walk.

At the Bronco, Tony waved him around to the passenger side and climbed in. They were all the way down to Conroy's main street before Gramp broke the silence. "So this is how narcs operate, hey?"

Tony was scanning the storefronts on both sides of the street and he answered almost absent-mindedly. "How what?"

"Separate the suspects."

"I don't know what the hell you're talking about," Tony said, nearly gritting his teeth. Before Gramp could say anything more he grunted, "Ha!" and angled the Bronco into one of the head-in parking places. He got out and said, "Come on."

They walked past a plate glass window painted with huge letters that said, "Olsen's Drugs & Novelties." Below that were smaller letters saying, "Books—Lending Library—Open Sun. Noon to 5."

Tony led Gramp into the store and looked around till he saw rows of books lining the back wall. With Gramp scooting along behind he hurried through the store to the back where he searched through the shelves of shiny, multi-colored dust jackets till he found what he wanted.

He pulled a book off its shelf, turned it over, and handed it to Gramp.

Gramp looked at the photograph on the dust jacket and then looked up at Tony. "That's you."

"Right."

"Sumbitch."

"Right. And that goes for JayDee, too. Let's try to step over this horseshit about me being a cop."

LATER THAT Sunday afternoon, Tony and Pat had a lot to talk about.

He'd taken Gramp back to the hospital, they'd all said goodbye to Jo, and Gramp had started back to the ranch in JayDee's pickup—"I'm drivin' his old junker while he tries to fix an oil leak in mine."

But watching the old man drive away, the first thing Pat said was "Thank you for giving me a chance to be alone with Jo. That poor girl still misses her mother, after all this time. She's been aching for someone to talk to."

"That sounds odd, since she lives with her father and her grandfather. And JayDee."

Pat turned a slight smile on her husband and said, "No offense, but there are times in life when men are not the answer." She paused, looking over the town toward the river canyon and the mountains. "Sometimes a man might be the last thing in the world a woman wants to see."

He paused for a few moments, too, then he nodded and they climbed into the car again and drove back toward the reservation while Pat talked about her conversation with Jo Miller.

Jo said that JayDee had convinced everyone at the Miller ranch that Tony was a policeman. And, as Jo told Pat quite seriously, ''JayDee's the only one we know who's ever gone to jail. So he oughta know.'' So they believed him.

Jo wasn't sure why JayDee had been sent to prison. He'd been in trouble for years. All the way through school, practically. She was three years behind him in school but she was always hearing stories about JayDee Hampton. Fighting, mostly. Or taking things. Somebody's lunch or school supplies, or food from the cafeteria. Even clothes. When he was a junior in high school, he went into the gym during the senior class play and took another boy's good suit. They kicked him out of school and he disappeared.

He went to Portland, the story was. A few years later there was a rumor that he'd been arrested and put in jail. Jo heard it was something about drugs and stealing a car. But she didn't know for sure.

Getting back to when they were in school, Jo told Pat another interesting little story. Almost every time JayDee got in trouble he'd show up at the Miller place afterwards.

Early in the morning, when Gramp or Win or Mrs. Miller went out to feed the chickens or milk or whatever, JayDee'd be there. Sleeping in the barn. And they'd get him straightened up. Get him something to eat. Get him back to town.

Nobody in the family knew how it started, or why. It was just something that was. But as much as he came around, there was never anything missing. Ever.

"I got basically the same story from Gramp," Tony said. "A little more detail, but not much."

"And I'm sort of skimming, because I want to tell you—" Pat stopped, seeming suddenly aware of her surroundings. They were driving south through Conroy, slowly. "Where'd all the cars come from? Did we hit the end-of-the-weekend traffic?"

Tony squirmed on the seat, looking ahead and back. "Guess so. You wanted to tell me what?"

All the time that Jo was talking about or answering questions about JayDee, Pat had the feeling that she wanted to talk more about her mother and father—her Momma, Jo called her. And Daddy.

Oh, how she misses her Momma. She still talks to her. After six years, she still talks to Momma when she has a problem. And she tries to hear the answers.

She mostly asks about Daddy. In that accident when Momma died he hurt his back so bad it's bothered him ever since. And it keeps getting worse. Doctors didn't seem to help and the bills were so high he stopped going. And gloomy? You never saw gloomy till you saw Daddy. And he was always such a happy man, before.

Then JayDee came back, paroled or something. He came to the ranch. Why he did, nobody knows. Sort of a second home, maybe.

So Daddy took him on and it wasn't long before Daddy started getting better. Working again, smiling again, everything seemed alright again. Then a few months ago it all went to hell again. Daddy's lost so much weight you can hardly see him.

Fact is, you hardly see him, anyway. Him and JayDee spend so much time back in those lava caves you'd think they were digging for gold or something. And when he does come to the house, he's almost like a stranger. Like a little old man. Looks older'n Gramp and acts like a stranger.

Pat's eyes filled with tears, repeating Jo's words, "'Why, oh why did Momma have to die? Why can't she help me know what to do?'" Tony reached across the seat to hold her hand. "Just before the accident, her mother took Jo to San Francisco and they went to the opera. Can you guess which one? *Madame Butterfly*. She still plays the record they bought afterward."

Pat wiped her eyes. She became conscious for the first time that their south-bound line of traffic had stopped. In the other lane, cars and trucks going north whooshed past Tony's left elbow so close that the air pressure whipped at his sleeve and rocked the Bronco.

He checked the mirrors and stuck his head out the window. In front and behind, not moving, stretched a long line of motor homes, campers, trailers, RVs, pickup trucks, and ordinary cars. They sat, at the same time dancing and shimmering, seeming to melt behind invisible waves of gas fumes and heat.

A few of the passengers and drivers got out of the waiting cars to walk and stretch on the shoulder of the road. They were all Indians.

"Who would have guessed it," Tony said, "a traffic jam in Central Oregon."

Pat slid back into the corner and stretched her legs across to Tony's side. "Might as well relax," she said, "while you tell me what Gramp had to say."

When Gramp looked at Tony's picture on the dust jacket of the book, the first thing he did was cuss. But at the same time he started to believe that JayDee was wrong about Tony being a narcotics cop.

Gramp thought maybe it was just natural for JayDee to think that way. Since it was a narc that put him in jail. And Gramp said that JayDee said that Tony acted the same as a narc. He just showed up one day, asking questions. And kept coming back, with more questions.

Gramp said that prob'ly the difference was that the only thing Tony asked about was shooting the TV. And the cattle. And what he'd need when he took the pictures. All the same, JayDee said, that's how narcs act at first. Like they're payin' no attention to what's going on.

So JayDee said. But Gramp had his own ideas as to why JayDee worried about cops nosin' round. And he checked 'em out. And there's gonna be hell to pay.

In the Bronco, wedged into the corner of her seat, Pat waited for Tony to go on with Gramp's story. Finally, she folded her arms across her chest and said, "Well? What was he 'checking out'?"

"He wouldn't say. In fact, he wouldn't say much more on that subject. But I got the feeling, somehow, that it had something to do with Win."

Pat pushed herself up, looking at the line of traffic as Tony let the Bronco roll forward a few feet. Far ahead she could see the long, slow column turning right under the flashing yellow light—motor homes, campers, pickups, pickups pulling trailers, RVs, and passenger cars loaded with families, dogs, clothes, food, and camping gear heading for the Short Falls Reservation.

"Is there a pow-wow coming up?"

"A big one—they call it Reservation Days. I'm not sure what it's all about."

"Guess we'll wait and see." Pat turned sideways on the seat. "Anyway, getting back to your talk with Gramp. What did he say about Win?"

"Not much. It was mostly about Win *and* JayDee."

Gramp opened his mouth. Closed it and opened it again and closed it again looking for the right words to say about JayDee. Finally he just said it was important to know about the kid's upbringing.

His daddy was a drunk. His momma was the next thing to a whore. He got beat, starved, and lied to from the time he was a tiny thing. People say Jay-

Dee's done some bad things. They say he's dangerous. Let me tell you.

People say the same thing about a yearling steer. But
you think on this. That steer got hurt every time a hu-
man touched him. Every time. You stuck those big
needles in him and gave him shots. You cut a notch out
of his ear. You dehorned him, you burnt a brand on
his ass, and you cut his balls off. Think he's gonna
come over and ask what else you got in mind?

JayDee, now. He's real touchy, just like that steer.
And shifty. That's why that Donna ain't gonna find
him. As good a rider as that gal is, where Win and
JayDee go ain't nobody gonna find 'em that don't
know the country.

Pat was sitting up, intent, her eyes going back and
forth from Tony to the intersection just ahead.
"Gramp said that Donna goes horseback riding on the
Miller place?"

Tony nodded. "Shooting, too."

Pat watched his profile. "You're joking."

"Gramp says she's out there almost every day. She
borrows a horse and a rifle—she brings her own
ammo—and goes for a ride and takes target practice."

"What on earth for?"

"Says it helps her relax." Tony glanced sideways at
Pat. "And guess who was missing from the location
when JayDee's horse got shot."

Pat let her head lay back on the top of the seat, thinking, and then she said quietly, her eyes closed, "Donna Hughes. Demon interpreter. Guardian of Japanese culture and protector of her lover, Dennis Shimada. Possible dingbat."

"Right."

After another short pause and with her eyes still closed Pat said, "Tony?"

"Yes?"

"Why don't you just stay at home and write?"

They'd reached the turnoff to the reservation where two police officers stood in the T-intersection under the blinking yellow light. One was an Oregon State Police trooper. Tony recognized the other as the Short Falls Reservation Tribal Policeman he'd talked to earlier, outside the chief's office.

The lines of cars seemed endless. Standing between the streams of traffic flowing both north and south, the two officers took turns directing cars onto Reservation Road.

Twenty or thirty at a time they rolled by with license plates showing they'd come here from every state in the western United States and Canada—Arizona, New Mexico, Colorado, Utah, Nevada, California, Oregon, Washington, Idaho, Montana, Wyoming, Alberta, British Columbia, Alaska.

Now at the front of this line, Tony waited for a signal from the tribal officer standing by his left front fender. Like the trooper's summer uniform, the tribal officer's short-sleeve suntans had creases that looked sharp enough to cut his fingers when he put it on. Like the trooper, he sheltered his eyes behind dark green aviator glasses. But unlike the trooper's his head was uncovered and his long black hair reflected flashes of sunlight as bright as the light that bounced off his glasses when he turned to look at Tony.

Tony stuck his head out the window and asked where everybody was going.

Before he answered, the officer backed along the side of the Bronco, thumbs tucked behind his wide belt, watching the trooper and the traffic. When he got to the door he recognized Tony and nodded. "Hi. People coming for Reservation Days."

"What's the background on that?"

Keeping an eye on the trooper the officer said, "The Short Falls Indian Confederation is made up of the Five Tribes. We signed a treaty a hundred and thirty years ago. The Five Tribes celebrate it every year.

"But this year's celebration is something special. *Big* celebration. Lots of people come. Wasco, Warm Springs, Paiute, Sioux, Yakima, Navajo, Flathead, lots more. This is only the beginning. By tomorrow there'll be so many people we'll have to make our 'money run' every day."

The trooper stopped the car coming north and pointed at the Bronco. The tribal officer said, "Okay, your turn" and stepped away to signal the line of cars behind Tony. "As long as you're here," he said, "you might wanta see the parade tonight. Pretty good show."

Tony put the Bronco in gear as he said, "Can Anglos go?"

"Sure," the officer called, "we're not prejudiced."

IT WAS EARLY in the evening but the music had already started. Loudspeakers blared the amplified beat of drums and a man's tight, keening chant as Tony and Pat walked through thick high grass across a field as big as a football field toward the weathered wood bleachers set up behind the Short Falls Community Center. They spotted some seats at the top of the six-row bleachers but before climbing through the crowd of townspeople and farmers, they stopped and looked around.

A flatbed trailer blocked off the right end of the lush green field. A microphone stand and judges' chairs had been set up on the trailer. In front of it, six men sat in a circle around their drums.

At the opposite end of the field and along the other side, charcoal smoke and cooking smells drifted up from an L-shaped row of pre-fab refreshment stands selling hot dogs, hamburgers, chili, and Indian fry bread.

Behind the flatbed trailer and the food stalls stood something Tony and Pat had never seen—acres and acres of tall white tepees. They ranged in a huge wide arc far beyond the grassy field, and as more visitors arrived more tepees were going up, their long thin poles poking up through the gathered tops of the high white canvas cones and into the afternoon's still-blue sky.

The tepees, much taller and wider than Tony had imagined, rose above a scattering of dome tents, wall tents, every kind of tent imaginable.

Hundreds of Indians meandered among the tepees and the tents and the food stalls, Indians in all shapes, sizes, and shades of color drinking Sprite and Coke out of paper cups, chewing hot dogs and pizza slices, licking sno-cones and Eskimo Pies. Slender mothers carried big-eyed babies in the crook of an arm or in a backpack. Boys and girls shuffled or ran around in caps and T-shirts that told the world they'd seen Disneyland or Knotts Berry Farm, the Raiders or the 49ers, or The Grateful Dead or The Eagles. Chatty round old women rolled by in straight-hanging shifts and sunglasses, following serious round old men in paunch-hugging knits and straw cowboy hats.

And stunning young men and women in their twenties and thirties sauntered casually through the crowd toward the judges' stand in their brilliantly colored ceremonial dress—eagle feathers, beaded breastplates, bone breastplates, fancy beaded cuffs, deerskin breechcloths and leggings, double bustles of dyed feathers rippling down their backs in cascades of color from lemon to vermilion, from pale blue to purple, beaded buckskin dresses, beaded embroidered shawls with long fringes sweeping the grass-tops, and bells.

Under the loud heavy amplified sounds, everyone heard the light jingling bells, the tiny bells sparkling down the legging seams, around the ankles, and on moccasin tops, the bells that made every step a ringing little song.

Pat touched Tony's arm and pointed to a four-year-old girl in beaded buckskin. "Look at that beautiful—"

He squeezed her hand hard and whispered, "Wait! Listen!" as a man climbing into the bleachers said to a neighbor, "—the Miller place. Don't know which one."

Tony touched the man's shoulder. "Excuse me, what was that about somebody at the Miller place?"

The man hardly looked at him. "One of 'em got killed."

SIXTEEN

Sunday (continued)

THE ROAD TO Nine Mountain Lake takes off west from Highway 97 between Conroy and Madras and runs along the north edge of the Miller property. By the time Tony and Pat got there the sun was low and the road was dark, but the bright spot in the road showed where the trouble was.

Spinning red-and-blue lights flashed from the overheads on a state police car and an ambulance. A few cars and pickups leaned at weird angles down the sloping shoulder of the road, some with their headlights on and some with just the yellow parking lights burning.

Tony held Pat's hand as they made their way through a small huddle of whispering, gossiping people, still wearing bathing suits, who were apparently on their way back from an afternoon at the lake.

They went around the open back door of the empty ambulance and stopped, shocked still. JayDee Hampton's yellow pickup was flipped upside down and rammed into the shallow slope on the other side of the ditch.

Tony put his arm around Pat's shoulders as they squinted in the glaring, garish light flicking over the truck's oily chassis and frame, over the hubless wheels, and over the jagged hole in the right front tire.

A split second later Pat saw the blood smeared on the ripped-open door of the truck and she gasped and ducked her head into Tony's shoulder. He held her tighter and started to turn. "Let's go on back to the car," he said, but just as they turned they nearly bumped into the emergency medical crew wrestling a rattling, squeaking gurney around the other side of the ambulance to the open door. The gurney's wheels chattered over rocks and weeds on the side of the road. The gurney shook so hard that the body on top, strapped under a blanket, seemed to be trying to shake itself free.

Tony and Pat sidestepped the medical crew and this time almost walked into Sergeant Kelsey. They stood still, as surprised to see the trooper as he was to see them. Finally, Tony was able to nod at the gurney being hoisted into the ambulance and say, "JayDee?"

The trooper shook his head. "Old man Miller."

They stared at him and Pat said, almost whispered, "Gramp?"

Kelsey nodded.

Pat's head rolled back as if she'd been hit. She stared up at the darkening sky. Tony looked down. Then silently they clung together, her head on his chest. With his arms around her, Pat cried. Tony looked at the ambulance door, swinging shut. His eyes were wet, too.

Kelsey said, "These guys worked on him for almost an hour. They really tried. But he was gone."

Still looking at the yellow door, Tony said, "What happened? Tire blow out?"

"Shot out."

They both looked at him, unbelieving, till Pat said, "Impossible." She stepped back, gazing up at Tony. "Who would do such a thing?—a wonderful old man like that?"

Before Tony could answer, Kelsey said, "I'd suggest that you folks go on back to The Lodge. There's nothing you can do here, and it would help get these other people moving."

He stopped, frowning at another car coming from the highway and crunching to a stop in the road. "Just what we need, more sightseers," he said. A pickup stopped on the other side of the road, apparently on its way back from Nine Mountain Lake.

Dennis Shimada got out of the passenger side of the car, and Donna Hughes came around from the driver's side. Across the road, a door slammed on the pickup.

"What happened?" Shimada asked Tony, squinting under the flashing lights. At the same time, holding her hands above her eyes, palms down, Donna asked Kelsey, "Is there anything we can do to help?" She shrugged. "Or should we just keep on going?"

Kelsey said, "Pretty late for a trip to the lake."

"A sunset pic—" Her mouth snapped shut and her eyes glared at JayDee Hampton storming up to Sergeant Kelsey.

"What the hell happened to my truck!" JayDee screamed. "Where the hell's Gramp!"

Donna slowly lowered her hands and the red-and-blue lights flashed over and over into her eyes as she looked at JayDee and at JayDee's truck upside down in the ditch and at Gramp Miller's truck on the other side of the road.

Tony nodded his head once to get Kelsey's attention. The officer was watching Donna.

"Has anyone told Win Miller about Gramp?" Tony asked quietly.

Kelsey shook his head. "He's not at the ranch. Nobody knows where he is."

SEVENTEEN

Monday

EARLY MONDAY MORNING a lone officer left the Short Falls Tribal Police Headquarters to collect the cash and checks taken in by the tribe's different businesses for deposit in the Conroy Bank—the money run. As usual, he drove a dark green Ford with the Tribal Police insignia somewhere under the dust on the front doors.

The officer started the run by driving down Reservation Road and across the river on the South Bridge. He picked up the cash bag at the Gift Shop and Information Center, at the intersection where the road joined Highway 97.

Next, he doubled back across the bridge to the Community Center. The two-girl office staff made him wait an extra fifteen minutes while they finished counting and bagging money from entry fees and refreshment stands at the Reservation Days celebration. But they gave him a second cup of coffee and two jelly doughnuts.

After wiping his fingers he dropped the Center's three bags and the Gift Shop bag into the trunk of his car and drove the reservation's Main Road to The

Lodge. At The Lodge he picked up two more bags, tossed them in with the others, and went back to the Main Road. At the junction there he turned left, also as usual, drove north on the Main Road, crossed the river on the North Bridge, and turned right onto Highway 97, settling back for the nineteen-mile run through Madras and on to Conroy.

The officer had barely got the Ford up to speed when a new red Chevrolet Corsica appeared in his rearview mirror out of nowhere, blasted its horn, and shot around in front of the police car. Muttering to himself—"Just cause we're not on the reservation, hey?"—the officer reached out his hand to flip on his overheads. "Maybe I'll shake this turkey up a little bit. 'Cause I bet he don't know I'm also a County Deputy."

But instead of flashing his lights he was suddenly grabbing the wheel with both hands, tapping his brakes, checking his mirror, because the Chevy had slowed. It was weaving back and forth across the yellow line, going slower and slower. Its flashers blinked on. The driver's left hand came creeping out the window, wagging weakly up and down.

The Chevy slowed even more, almost came to a stop in the middle of the highway. The officer punched on his own overheads, tapping his brakes and staying with the Chevy. In tandem, the two cars eased over to the right shoulder of the road.

"Must be a brand new car. No stickers anywhere. Clean bumpers. Clean windows. Nothing on the back shelf. New Car. Or a rental." The officer strained for a look at the driver through the Chevy's rear window. All he could see was the top of the head—perhaps a little old man or woman scrunched way down in the seat. Whoever it was was so short he had to look through the steering wheel.

The two cars thumped across a wooden culvert and down a little dirt road toward the river and a public boat ramp. Between the road and the river lay a small oval of cleared ground surrounded by a stand of willows that blocked the view from the launch below and the highway above.

The Chevy stopped, motor still running, lights still flashing. The driver's arm snaked slowly out the window again, sagged, and dropped against the door, limp.

The officer jumped out of his car and rushed forward to help the stricken driver. At the driver's door, he looked through the window and straight down the large round, black barrel of a shotgun.

The officer stared. A muffled voice said, "On the ground. Face down. Fast."

But the officer simply stood there, frozen, staring at a Ronald Reagan mask.

Bloodshot eyes peered through the eyeholes, not blinking. The muffled voice came out of the mask again. "I'll kill you."

The officer dropped to the ground, face down. The man in the Ronald Reagan mask slid out of the car. He knelt on one knee, resting the shotgun barrel on the officer's shoulder, the muzzle in his ear. He slipped the officer's .357 Magnum out of its holster and lifted his two speedloaders and a pair of handcuffs off his belt. He cuffed the officer's hands behind his back, dropped the gun and speedloaders into the Chevy, pulled a length of rope from his own hip pocket, and tied the officer's feet.

The Ronald Reagan mask hurried to the police car, turned off the motor, yanked the keys out, and went back to the trunk. He opened the trunk, grabbed the six money bags and then dropped three as a loud voice bellowed over a bullhorn, "Cut-oh! Cut!"

The Ronald Reagan mask jerked and turned, looking frantically around, waving the shotgun with one hand and trying to pick up the money bags with the other. He couldn't find a source for the voice. He got all the money bags together in his arms again.

The voice roared, "Check-u!" and he dropped two bags. The Ronald Reagan mask peered into the willow trees. Toward the road. Toward the river. The bound policeman. The sky. Nothing.

The Ronald Reagan mask stuffed the shotgun under an armpit and snatched up the bags with both hands. He cradled the bags in his arms and scurried to the Chevy. He slung the money bags inside. He ran back to the police car and yanked out the radio wires. He started around the car to close the trunk.

The voice boomed, "Check-u okay!" The Ronald Reagan mask shook no-no-no, scooted to the Chevy, and spun it in a dust-flying U-turn toward the road as the camera truck came backing slowly up the boat ramp behind the willows, with Tony standing on the platform top alongside the cameraman.

The policeman yelled as the Chevy squealed up the road toward the highway. Tony and the cameraman turned and saw the Chevy, the police car, the open trunk, the officer on the ground.

Tony pointed at the red car. The cameraman swiveled his camera around, focused on the rear end of the car, and read the license plate out loud.

Then he panned up the car, stopped, and jerked away from his viewfinder. There was no expression on his face but his eyebrows lifted about two inches.

He looked at Tony and said, "The President-u?"

EIGHTEEN

Monday Afternoon

"THE CAR and the license number you gave me don't go together. We found that out real fast."

Sheriff Eldon Cooper raised his iced tea glass out of a little puddle of water on the restaurant counter and swabbed at the puddle with the flat of his other hand. "The plates were stolen off a car parked at Portland International."

He looked at Tony, seated on the stool beside him. "And we found out the car was rented there at the airport, too. Thanks to you. How'd you know that?"

"I didn't." Tony reached across the counter and tugged a paper napkin out of its metal box. He handed it to the sheriff. "I just made a suggeston."

"Well, we found it. And faster than we might've." Cooper wiped his hand with the napkin and then wiped the counter. "It was rented from Budget. By a 'W. Miller.'"

Surprised, Tony sat straight up, eyeing the sheriff. "Win Miller?"

But Cooper shrugged and said, "Iced tea is more trouble than it's worth sometimes. My doctor wants me to cut back on coffee. That's the only reason I'm drinking it." He looked at Tony. "Why am I telling you this stuff?"

Tony relaxed again. "Maybe I look like your doctor?"

"I mean the police stuff."

"Because I bribed you with a piece of peach pie and a sloppy glass of tea."

"That's it. You're under arrest."

"Because I reported the robbery, with the Short Falls officer. And because I suggested calling companies like Budget before trying the big ones."

"Ah. You're free to go, then." The sheriff mashed the back of his fork down onto the few remaining crumbs of pie crust, shoved them in his mouth, put the fork on the plate, and pushed the plate away.

As Cooper performed his clean-up operation Tony reminded him, "The Short Falls officer is the one who thought the car might be a rental. I just hitchhiked on his idea and said to start small."

The sheriff nodded. "Sounded kind of funny, both of you."

"Well, if the *car* wasn't local, wouldn't the *driver* have to be somebody from around here? Wouldn't he or she have to be a local, to know about the money run? And when? And where?"

Cooper turned a little and leaned his elbow on the short back of the wood stool. "And?"

"And if it's a local. In a rented car. With license plates stolen from a car at the airport. Maybe that's where he rented a red Chevy."

"But why call the smaller companies? Why not—"

"I know a lot of people who use Hertz or Avis. On their expense accounts. But when they're spending their own money..."

Tony left the thought in mid-air.

Cooper nodded. "Got it."

Tony dug some money out of his jeans, left enough for the bill and a tip, and walked with the sheriff toward the front door.

Outside, they stood under the awning's shade and Tony said, "If I'm not pressing my luck, can you tell if you're looking for Win?"

The sheriff didn't answer right away. Then, "I can tell you that nobody we know has seen him."

"If you were looking for him, do you have any idea about how long it'd take?"

"Do you have any idea how big this country is?" Before Tony could answer, Cooper answered himself. His voice didn't sound angry, merely tired of counting numbers that were out of proportion. "Reducing it to round figures, two thousand square miles. I have me, an undersheriff, a narcotics investigator, a crime scene investigator, three patrol sergeants, and eight patrol deputies. For two thousand square miles. Might take a while."

Tony let a couple of seconds pass, absorbing the numbers. "Okay. Have you heard any more about Gramp?"

Cooper's head swung from side to side and he looked down. He kicked an invisible rock and the sole of his shiny black boot scraped the sidewalk. His voice was soft when he finally said, "Poor old bastard. What a shame."

Tony's eyes searched his face. "He wasn't shot, was he? I thought it was the tire."

"Oh, yes. Somebody shot out the tire. Gramp just rolled around inside that truck while it turned over and broke his neck. Might've been better if he *was* shot." Cooper raised his head, squinting at the sun's bright reflections off the few cars and trucks passing on the wide street.

He took a deep breath and his voice brightened as he jerked a thumb over his shoulder and asked Tony, "See that sign?"

Peering past him, Tony saw a poster taped in the restaurant window.

Cooper said, "Those signs are all over town, and every time I see one I'm gonna think of old man Miller."

Tony read the first line out loud. "Barlow County Fair and Rodeo—4-H and FFA Sale." Special events were listed under the headline. Cow-Cutting Contest. Open Cow Horse Contest. Quick Draw Charlie. Elk's

Buckaroo Breakfast. Tractor and Four-By-Four Pull. Senior Citizens Potluck.

While Tony scanned the poster Cooper said, "Old Gramp loved the County Fair. And I'll tell you something. Now—today—even at his age, he'd win that cow-cutting contest." He laughed, a kind of snort. "Tell you something else. He wouldn't be caught *dead* at that 'senior citzens' deal. Know what he called it? 'Potty luck.'" He suddenly swiped the grin off his face and kicked at the sidewalk again. "Shit," he said. "Thanks for the pie." And he walked away.

PAT HAD BEEN at the hospital for more than an hour, sitting in a chair by Jo's bed, holding her hand, talking about Gramp. Jo told tender stories, grouchy stories, forgetful stories.

Listening to the stories, talking about him, Pat began to feel as though she'd been Gramp's friend for years. She found herself nodding, knowing. She could see him in the house or the barn or the shed, on a tractor or on a horse. So Jo talked, and Pat listened, and even the funny stories made them cry.

After a while the silence between the stories began to grow longer and they'd just sit together, tears in their eyes, hand softly stroking hand.

Finally, Pat said, "I think I'd better go so you can rest, now. Maybe a little nap."

She stood and moved around to the other side of the bed as Jo said, "Don't go. Maybe Daddy'll come today. Maybe you'll finally get to meet him."

Pat started to say something but she hesitated, her gaze drifting across the bed to the chair where she'd been sitting and on out the window.

Watching her, Jo said, "What is it? What were you going to say?"

After a deep breath, Pat said, "Well, you'll have to hear it from someone." She looked into Jo's eyes. "I'm sorry I'm the one. But there was a robbery. A lot of money was taken. The police think your father may be involved."

Jo frowned. Every trace of friendship drained from her face. She glared at Pat and neither of them knew the nurse had come in the room with a glass pitcher full of ice cubes. Walking toward the bed and looking all around the room she said, "Where'd he go?"

Jo was still glaring at Pat, but Pat looked at the nurse. "Where'd who go?"

Dumping ice into Jo's water carafe, the nurse glanced at her and said, "Your dad."

Jo's head spun around and she almost shouted, "Daddy?"

"He was right outside your door. I took ice across the hall and he was standing there. I came out, gone." On her way out she said, "Maybe he went to the john."

Pat waited a silent minute after the nurse had gone. "Well," she said, "please don't shoot the messenger. I'd still like to be your friend." She stood in the cold silence for another few moments and then walked away, leaving Jo staring out the window.

A minute later, still staring out the window, Jo saw her daddy cross the parking lot a half-step behind Pat Pratt and then push her into his pickup.

NINETEEN

Monday Evening

LAST night Donna Hughes couldn't explain to Dennis
Shimada why she suddenly called off their picnic and
drove straight back to The Lodge. Or why she left him
in the lobby and went up to her room, grim and alone.

And she didn't tell him that she sat there in the dark,
huddled in a chair, staring through her open window
into the stars until they washed away in the chill
morning light.

But on Monday she told Shimada that she was ready
for another excursion. Their shooting schedule was
almost finished, she said. She thought they should use
their last few days in America to see as much as possible of this big, raw country. Then they could return
to Japan strengthened in their dedication to the culture, the dignity, and the serenity of that small country they both love.

One of the sights she wanted to see was sunset
glowing on the mountains and the river; shadows
darkening one wall of the broad deep canyon while the
other side burns red with light; the shadows slowly
darkening down the coulee walls, to violet, to purple,
then a sudden plunge to cold black at the bottom

while, above, warm slanting yellow light still warms the horizontal earth.

So when the crew set out in the late afternoon to set up for a night scene in the woods near the North Bridge and the production caravan turned left past the bridge, Donna Hughes and Dennis Shimada turned right. They drove south through Madras toward the viewpoint road above the Short Falls River.

JayDee Hampton happened to be in Madras at the same time, riding in a red Cadillac. The Cadillac turned slowly out of the driveway toward Main, gliding into the sparse Monday evening traffic one car behind the station wagon.

At the viewpoint, the station wagon and the Cadillac were the only two cars that turned into the parking area. Shimada followed Donna's direction and turned right, proceeding thirty yards to a low wall of rough brown basalt, stained and faded old rocks that had been scraped up and stacked there to form the north boundary when the viewpoint was built.

Approaching the rocks he made a sharp left turn and stopped, his front bumper almost touching the low guardrail that ran along the canyon side of the viewpoint and ended at the rocks. Three feet past the guardrail the canyon dropped twelve hundred feet.

By the time Dennis Shimada stopped, Donna was looking back nervously, the sunset forgotten. The only other car at the viewpoint was close behind, following in their tracks.

The Cadillac pulled parallel to the station wagon and then backed up, swinging behind the wagon's rear bumper, forming a T.

JayDee jumped out and ran to Donna's door, screaming curses, his face twisted, furious, eyes bulging. "You shot my truck, you tried to kill me! But you killed the old man! You shot the old man, you stupid bitch! You! It was you! I know it was you!"

He jerked the door open, grabbed her arm and a fistful of her hair as she screeched, "No, no, Dennis, help me!" She kicked, flailed, and tried to bite as he hauled her out of the car.

Shimada sat stunned for a second by JayDee's fury, not understanding his assault on Donna. Then he leaped out and tried to get around the back to help.

The Cadillac blocked his way and the slick-haired man sat behind the steering wheel shaking his head. He held up his left hand, palm out, and pointed a pistol at Shimada with his right. "Best for you to stay out of it," he said.

Shimada spun and ran to the front of the station wagon and rolled across the hood. Landing on his feet he dove into the hurricane of feet, fists, screams, and flashing teeth.

Somehow he got between JayDee and Donna. He shoved JayDee away. But JayDee grabbed Shimada, spun him around, and drove his right fist into Shimada's face. Falling back, Shimada grabbed JayDee's arm and a fistful of shirt.

They tumbled against the rock wall in a clinch, knocking the top layers of rock loose, wrestling, scattering the big stones. Some dropped down the back side, a few scraped and rolled down the front.

In the noise of the fight—Donna screaming, the men grunting and yelling, their feet scuffling and scraping on the gravel—nobody noticed the excited rattle of the snakes exposed by the tumbling, shifting rocks.

Shimada got a fist free and drove JayDee back. JayDee spun him around and Shimada stumbled backward past Donna and thudded against the door of the station wagon. JayDee came after him, ignoring Donna. Behind JayDee, she picked up a rock. She swung it at the back of his head but her foot slipped in the scree and debris. Instead of a knockout it was merely a glancing blow that wrenched the rock out of her hand, but it made him duck with pain and turn his head to see where it came from.

As JayDee looked around, Shimada drove a fist into his belly and made him stagger back. At the same time, Donna reached behind her to grab another rock, this one off the wall. Her fingers fell on a rock too big for one hand. She twisted around and grabbed it with both hands and for the first time she saw the snakes.

She screamed a horrible scream as a frightening flat head shot out of the rocks and those hideous jaws snapped into her skin on the back of her left wrist. Another rattlesnake struck the inside of her right wrist. A third snake flicked up from the front of the wall and sank his fangs into her throat.

Still screaming, she whirled away from the wall, her face a terrified white mask, with all three snakes hanging, wriggling, whipping from her body. Her wild endless screams pealed off the canyon walls. Her eyes filled with as much hate as fear, she charged at JayDee, swinging her arms, beating at her chest.

He backed away.

She kept coming, arms waving.

He tripped backwards over the guardrail.

The snakes released from her arms.

Even as he fell he watched them squirm through the air.

Donna kept coming, the rattler dangling from her neck.

JayDee tried to scramble to his feet, still crawling backward.

Donna fell over the guardrail. She hit the ground. Her screams turned to choking whimpers.

The rattler bounced free, scuttling toward JayDee. JayDee jumped up. He took one step backward and dropped off the rim of the canyon. As he fell toward the rocks more than a thousand feet below, his scream echoed Donna's.

Before the echo died, Shimada knelt by Donna's side. The slick-haired man crouched over them. "We'll carry her to my car," he said. There was no question in his voice. "If you've got any coats or blankets in the station wagon, bring 'em. Let's go. And keep her as quiet as you can.''

They stretched her on the back seat of the Cadillac, covered her with every sweater and jacket they could find, and raced for the Conroy hospital.

Dennis Shimada half-sat, half-knelt beside her, holding her hand. She seemed to sleep, but at one point she said, ''Dennis?'' Her eyes stayed closed.

''Yes. I'm here. Stay quiet, please.''

In Conroy, the car was climbing the hill to the hospital when she stirred again. ''Dennis, is JayDee driving?''

''No.''

''Where is JayDee?''

Shimada hesitated. ''He is dead.''

Her head rolled a little to one side and a smile started on her lips, then faded. ''Did I shoot him?''

''No.''

The slick-haired man turned his head enough to ask, ''Did you try?''

''Yes.''

''Why?''

Her eyes flickered and she squeezed Shimada's hand. ''I was afraid for you. He might try to hurt you.'' She was silent. Then, ''I'm so sorry Mr. Miller died.''

The slick-haired man turned again. ''Did you shoot his horse?''

A frown moved over the pale skin between her closed eyes. After another silence she said, "No. I could never shoot a horse."

As the red Cadillac swung up to the hospital's emergency entrance she asked, "If that isn't JayDee, who's driving?"

Shimada shrugged as the slick-haired man jumped out and ran inside for help. But it was too late.

Dennis Shimada waited in the Cadillac for the slick-haired man to take him back to get the station wagon. But instead of driving to the viewpoint, the slick-haired man drove into Conroy and stopped at a corner on Main Street.

"Sorry, but I can't take you to your car," the slick-haired man said. "Something else has come up."

He pointed to a big stone building a block away. "The sheriff's office is in there," he said. "They'll be able to get you to your car. And while you're there, you might want to tell 'em what I just heard at the hospital.

"They said Mrs. Pratt was kidnapped by Win Miller late this afternoon and taken away in a red Chevrolet. Jo Miller was a witness but she didn't say anything till just a little while ago. It was her daddy, she said. She didn't know what to do.

"You tell 'em that in the sheriff's office. Maybe they can get in touch with Mr. Pratt through the State Police."

TWENTY

Monday Night

AT DUSK, Tony stood beside the camera truck at the edge of a narrow gravel road running through a pine forest a half-mile off the reservation's Main Road. He stuffed himself into his parka while he watched the TV crew set up for a night shoot.

A few men laid a line of four-by-six sheets of plywood along the side of the road. Other men came along right behind them connecting long lengths of aluminum together like narrow railroad tracks and laid them down on the plywood for the camera dolly to roll on.

Still others strung long, black electric cables from a portable generator to two giant floodlights and several spotlights on tall stands ranged behind and on each end of the camera track.

In this scene the boy Norio is lost and alone in the woods at night after becoming separated from his uncle, played by Dennis Shimada, following their raft ride on the river. They'd already shot the scene in which the boy and his uncle find each other; now they were setting up a series of dolly shots showing the boy, cold and frightened, wandering through the dark and nearly impenetrable forest.

Tony felt a movement by his side. Sergeant Kelsey was pulling on his state police parka over his uniform.

Motioning toward Norio huddling under a blanket on the seat of the camera truck, Tony said, "Won't have any trouble looking cold tonight." He had to raise and project his voice over the noisy, chuffing generator. Little clouds of breath followed his words and floated for a second in the chill night air.

Kelsey nodded. "This time of year we usually get about a fifty-sixty degree temperature swing. Got up close to a hundred today and we'll get down about forty tonight."

"Feels colder."

They stood together a few minutes, watching the crew. Kelsey's portable radio was holstered on a hip near Tony. Every now and then it sputtered static and a woman's high, nearly unintelligible voice. Tony glanced at the officer. "You've been working almost every day I've been here. Aren't you about due for a day off?"

"This is it." Kelsey didn't take his eyes off the crew.

Tony leaned against the corner of the truck. "You took this night duty on your day off?"

Kelsey kept watching the crew. "I got *assigned* this night duty on my day off." He looked back at Tony. "As I told you before, everybody in the state wants to take care of these TV people. It comes down from the governor to the superintendent to the station commander to me. So here I—'' His radio crackled again.

Despite the static and the rumbling generator Tony made out the words ''Kelsey'' and ''Miller'' and ''hospital.'' He pushed himself away from the van. ''What was that?''

Kelsey jerked the radio out of the holster and held it close to his mouth to answer the call. Then he slid it back into the holster. ''I'm going to the car where I can hear better. You might wanta come along.''

The officer turned to his car parked across the road about fifty feet from the camera truck. Tony followed after him, slowly, hands stuffed in the back pockets of his jeans.

Away from the oval of lights ringing the camera dolly, the night was surprisingly dark. He looked up. The broad sky was nearly black, but sparkling with so many stars that it seemed almost crowded. ''Like an ocean sky,'' he muttered. The generator's noise was masked a little by distance and the trucks around.

Behind the open door of the white Oregon State Police car, Kelsey sat sideways on the driver's seat, one boot on the door frame, the other on the gravel road. With the door open, the dome light was on but the broad brim of Kelsey's hat kept his face in shadow.

As Tony walked up he heard Kelsey ask his dispatcher, ''Is that an order?'' After a pause the answer came back, ''Yessir.''

Kelsey stretched his arm across the top of his steering wheel, his hand wrapped around the microphone. He gripped it so hard that his knuckles turned white, then he raised the mike to his mouth. "Who's covering the Miller place?"

"Anderson's leading. And a backup's on the way from Bend. And it's possible—repeat, *possible*—from what the civilian said, that Paulsen is on his way there, too."

"Roger," Kelsey said. "Please keep me informed."

"Ten-four. Nine-oh-seven P.M."

The radio went silent. Kelsey clipped his mike in place. He shoved himself out of the car and stood with his arms on the top of the open door, looking at Tony on the other side. "Mr. Pratt, I have to tell you that there's a rumor—an unconfirmed report—about your wife."

Tony's hands dropped to his sides and then he stood very still. Kelsey hesitated and Tony said, "Speak! Spit it out!"

Kelsey's voice was a monotone, mechanical. "There's a report that Win Miller took her from the hospital earlier today."

"'Took her'? What the hell does *that* mean!"

"He forced her into a car and took off."

"Where! The Miller place? Is that what you meant?—'who's covering the Miller place'?"

He didn't wait for an answer.

WHEN HE GOT THERE he turned off his headlights and let the Bronco roll along the bumpy driveway to stop under the big willow. He sat, still and quiet, looking and listening. The house, the shed, and the barn looked calm and peaceful in the starlight. A peacock screeched and almost stopped his heart. A single hollow yap came from inside the closed house.

Then, down by the barn, just for an instant, a light flashed. Tony stared. It came again, a quick streak of vertical light. And again.

He drove slowly toward it, his head swiveling, eyes squinting, trying to see anything and everything. The Bronco rocked down into the barnyard where the starlight glinted off the red Cadillac convertible. Beyond it loomed the big black square of the open barn door.

Tony stopped behind the Cadillac. He turned off his engine. The quiet was intense, and then the light flashed again a few feet straight ahead. It came from the car, from the driver's side. The door was ajar, opening and closing just enough to turn on the interior light at the bottom. But the car was empty.

He opened his own door, quietly. He stepped down. He started carefully toward the convertible. There was a groan and he stopped and the light flickered long enough to glimpse a foot pushing against the inside of the door.

Tony hurried to the door and looked in and then looked away quickly from the bloody mess sprawled across the front seat. It was the slick-haired man. His left shoulder was ripped open, blown all over the seat and the rest of the car, probably by a shotgun.

He appeared to be barely alive, shivering and shaking from the cold and probably from shock. But he was still moving, struggling to reach something on the floor of the car, and with his efforts his foot kicked at the door, moving it just enough to make the light flash on.

Tony took a deep breath, pulled the door open, and looked inside. The man was reaching weakly for a blood-spattered radio exactly like Sergeant Kelsey's.

Tony saw some sweaters and jackets on the back seat of the Cadillac. He grabbed a couple and spread them over the slick-haired man. The man stopped moving and looked at Tony. "Who you?" he muttered.

Leaning into the car Tony said, "My name is Pratt. Tony Pratt. Who're you?"

"Paulsen. Anybody else comin'?" He shivered.

"State troopers."

"Ah. All right."

"What happened?"

"Miller."

"Win Miller shot you?"

The slick-haired man's body shook in a violent shudder before he nodded and whispered. "Shotgun. Your wife. Miller. Took her to cave."

"Up the trail behind the barn? About a quarter-mile?"

"You know?"

"If I'm guessing right. Above the valley? Two big boulders with a juniper between 'em?"

The slick-haired man was nodding feebly. "Right."

"I knew it." Tony slapped the top of the door. He pushed himself out of the Cadillac and stood up.

"Don't go!" The man said it like giving an order.

"What?"

"Let troopers do it."

Tony said, "No time," and started to leave.

"Wait!" Tony leaned back into the car. "Take my piece," the man said. "On the steering post."

Groping below the steering wheel Tony said, "'Piece'? The only people who call a gun a 'piece' are military or police." He felt a gun, clipped to the post. "Are you a cop?" He stood up holding a Smith and Wesson revolver.

The slick-haired man didn't answer. Instead he said, "He's got the tribal officer's piece. And two speed-loaders. That's eighteen shots. And a shotgun."

TWENTY-ONE

Monday Night (continued)

PAT WAS SCARED to death. The skinny little man leaning against the cave wall scared her spitless. He'd looked bad enough in the daytime—skin and bones in baggy overalls—but in the shaky light from a stubby little emergency candle he was frightening.

She couldn't believe who he was. "Jo's daddy," he'd said, after he'd grabbed her and shoved her in the truck at the hospital. "Gramp's boy," he'd giggled. "Imagine callin' your own daddy 'Gramp'?"

Jo had said... Poor Jo. "When JayDee first came back Daddy got better," she'd said. "Then he got worse. Now you wouldn't know him."

The way he walked and held his shoulders showed a trace of Gramp. And the shape of the eyes and the nose showed a trace of Jo. But...

Pat shuddered. She couldn't see either Gramp or Jo in there any more.

Skinny, wrinkled, filthy. Shivering and sweating at the same time. He was fifteen feet away and she could smell him. When he walked by it was worse. When he tied her feet together she almost gagged.

And the shotgun. He looked so weak it was a wonder he could hold it. It looked too heavy. The barrel was thicker than his arm. But he never let go of it except for when he tied her feet, never put it down after he shot the man in the Cadillac.

God, that was awful! Hideous! Pat tugged the greasy cotton blanket tighter around her shoulders and shivered again but it wasn't from the cold.

THEY'D BEEN in the barn. Win Miller had driven his pickup into a wide stall inside the barn and parked beside a red Chevrolet. He'd got out, leaving Pat in the truck with her hands tied to the door handle.

He went to the front of the truck, kicking tin cans out of the way and cursing JayDee. "Didn't fix the goddamn oil leak like he said. Didn't bring me the stuff like he said. Left it in his gas can and now it's gone and I'm out. Empty. And I need some."

He opened a can of oil and while it drained into the engine he went to the red car and leaned inside.

Pat was nervous and scared but when he stood up and turned around she almost laughed. There in the barn was a short, skinny, stinking little Ronald Reagan. With a shotgun and a pistol.

With the mask on he scuttled back to the trunk and started throwing money bags into the back of the truck, all the time cackling and giggling and doing a crazy little dance like Walter Huston in *Treasure of the Sierra Madre*.

Suddenly he stopped, snatched off the mask and flung it down, grabbed the shotgun and aimed it across the bed of the truck. Pat turned and looked through the open barn door.

A red Cadillac convertible had pulled across the opening and the slick-haired man behind the wheel called in to Miller, "Hey, man, what's happening?" He sounded casual but he carefully kept his hands on top of the steering wheel.

"I'm the man JayDee deals with. Could you point that gun someplace else?"

"It ain't loaded."

"Right. That's the kind that kills people."

"Here, I'll show you." Miller snapped the shotgun to his shoulder, aimed at the man ducking under his dashboard, and pulled the trigger.

The hammer clicked. Miller let out a high-pitched giggle. "What'd I tell you?"

As the slick-haired man sat up and ran his palms over his head Miller jammed three shells into his shotgun. "Loaded now, though. Grab that steering wheel."

The man wrapped his hands, side by side, around the top of his steering wheel, his fingers flexing and straightening.

Miller let the barrel drift toward the Cadillac's windshield. "You got some stuff?"

"I gave it to JayDee. You got my money?"

"I gave it to JayDee."

"Looks like we both got a problem."

"How's that?"

"JayDee's dead."

"That wasn't him in his truck, that was my old man."

"JayDee dropped off a cliff today."

"You shittin' me?"

"No."

"Shit."

"Right."

Miller licked his lips and moved the shotgun to point a little more toward the man. "You got some stuff?"

"I told you. No."

"JayDee said you always kept some in that car."

"He was wrong. But I can get some."

"Where?"

"In town."

"How soon?"

"Now."

"How much?"

"Tell you what. You say you already paid JayDee?"

"I did."

"Okay, that means I owe you a delivery. So I'll go get it and bring it right back."

Miller licked his lips again. "Don't sound like your way to do business. 'Cash only,' JayDee always said you said."

"Tell you what. You got that woman, right?"

"Right."

"Okay, I bring you some stuff and you give me the woman."

Miller's high-pitched "Hee-hee" sounded strange. "Me, too."

"What?"

"Kinda good-lookin', ain't she? Bet she's more'n a one-hump camel, too."

"*Now* I know why you took her."

After a quick glance toward Pat, Miller scratched his crotch and giggled again. "It's a thought. So I'll keep her."

"So it *is* why you took her."

Miller wet his lips and his face turned serious. "She told my girl that the cops guessed I robbed the Indian cop. So she's my hostage. They come after me, I got her to bargain with."

"You can bargain with me right now. You can trade her for a lot o' stuff."

"How much?"

"Enough for a couple o' weeks. A month. You could have it in twenty minutes."

"You sure you ain't got some right there? And keep your hands up on that steering wheel."

"Positive. But I can get some. Fast."

"JayDee also said you kept a gun in there, too." Miller walked around the bed of his truck.

In the cab, looking back over her left shoulder, Pat saw Win Miller approach the driver's door of the Cadillac. He held his shotgun in both hands low across his body. The slick-haired man dropped his left hand down and opened the door. His left foot reached out for the ground and his right hand stretched under the steering wheel as Miller's shotgun exploded.

Faster than Pat could close her eyes, the man's shoulder disappeared in a blast of flame, smoke, and blood.

TREMBLING, SWEATING, Miller let the shotgun dangle from his left hand, leaning his right shoulder against the cave wall beside the narrow head-high opening. "Poor JayDee, damn his ass."

Miller's high thin voice, bouncing off the cold stone wall, seemed to Pat to come from another place, remote and unreal.

"But he may be better off, if he's really dead like that guy said. Cops'd get him, sooner or later, buyin' stuff for me. Well"—he looked at Pat—"*that* guy was a cop. You saw him." Pat shuddered and buried her face in her hands and the filthy blanket. "Yeah. You saw him." He turned away. "Took me back to Korea. That's where I got on the stuff the *first* time. Get your ass shot off and get doped for the pain and stay doped to forget it."

Miller's teeth started chattering. He clamped his mouth shut and shuffled the twenty feet to where the top of the cave curved down to a long, narrow slot. His scrawny, hunched-over body moving past the candle cast a grotesque shadow up the wall and across the ceiling.

He turned and stumbled back, standing on the other side of the slot, his back to Pat.

"Nobody around here knew that, though. Not even my old man. But he got to figurin' it out, after JayDee came back and started gettin' me 'medicine' for my crummy back. He got to know what JayDee was doin'. And me. Smart old man, my old man."

Miller sat on the floor with the shotgun by his side and hugged his bony knees to his bony chest. "But the only way he could figure to stop it was to stop JayDee. Not me. JayDee." He was still for almost a minute. He started rocking, slowly. "So one day up here when I was tied up out o' my head, he tries to shoot him from up here, thinkin' that that fake stampede'd chew up the body and nobody'd ever know what happened." He sat quietly. "That JayDee. Poor little bastard. All he was doin' was tryin' to help me. The only way he knew how."

He rolled over on the floor of the cave and curled himself into a ball, sobbing. Tears were rolling down Pat's face, too, when Tony slid through the narrow opening holding the slick-haired man's gun in both hands.

Epilogue

ONE WEEK LATER the TV production was all wrapped up.

The cast and crew celebrated with an incredibly long, loud, and stupefying party during which one of Portland's finest Japanese restaurants was nearly dismantled. The next day they bought every aspirin and icepack in town and crawled aboard a Delta Airlines flight to Tokyo.

Tony and Pat Pratt returned to their quiet suburban Lakewood home just a few miles south of Portland, their major concern for the moment being to help Jenny and Dan get ready for the next college term. And to figure out how to get their stuff down to the University of Oregon and to Oregon State in as few trips as possible.

Win Miller was in jail.

The slick-haired man he shot, narcotics investigator Walt Paulsen, was expected to recover after extensive surgery and rehabilitation on his shoulder.

Win hadn't been charged with kidnapping. Pat refused to pursue it. "Enough is enough," she said.

Jo Miller was out of the hospital and back at the ranch, sad and lonesome. An aunt and uncle came over from Pendleton to help out while she decided what to do—whether to sell the place, lease it, or try to run it herself.

Two weeks after the end of production Tony got a phone call from director Nobu Okumura in Tokyo. Nobu thanked him for his help and said that the final picture came together beautifully. Everyone at the company was pleased and grateful.

Three weeks after that, Tony and Pat drove back to Central Oregon to complete some unfinished business—a long, quiet weekend together. They played, they played, they swam, they went horseback riding, and they played.

And Pat went to see Jo Miller. She'd decided to stay on the ranch, Jo told Pat. "I remember Daddy and Momma talking about it. Gramp, too. 'This's been "The Miller place" for four generations,' they'd say. They used to talk about makin' it five, maybe even ten. So I guess I'll try."

On the Monday morning of their long weekend, Tony kept a long-deferred golf date with Father James J. McCuddy of St. Michael's Church in Conroy.

On another Monday morning several weeks earlier, Tony had rushed into Conroy, captured Father Mac, and taken him far out into the country to bless the Japanese crew on their first day of shooting. As a way of saying thank you, he'd promised to treat the priest to a game of golf at The Lodge.

So now, Tony was introducing Pat to Father Mac under the Spanish olive tree near the first tee.

Following the introductions, Father Mac looked all around Pat and said, "No clubs? You're not playing?"

"No, I don't play. But if you don't mind, I'll accompany."

"Of course, of course. But you're most certainly welcome to play. Your game can't be any worse than mine."

"Thank you, no. I'm in complete agreement with the old saying that golf ruins a nice walk in the country."

Father Mac smiled at Pat and turned to Tony. "A mind of her own."

"Yes, indeed."

After a few practice swings while the twosome ahead teed off, Father Mac and Tony walked on toward the tee. "Do you have some other work to do in films? With this Japanese group?"

"Not with the Japanese group, no. By an odd coincidence, though, my next job is with another foreign company. Recording some television sound tracks."

"Oh?"

"Yes," Pat said with a smile. "We're going to England. Isn't that exciting?"

"It is indeed! But, do you mean that you'll be recording English actors for American television?"

"No, no," Tony said, "we'll take an American actor along." He glanced at Pat. "Did I tell you? The client has decided to take Paul Taylor."

Pat stopped in her tracks. Tony and Father Mac walked on a couple of steps before they realized they'd left her behind. They turned and looked back. She stared at Tony. "*Not* Paul Taylor."

"Yes."

"No."

"Sorry."

They went on to the first tee as the priest said to Pat, "I gather this is a person you don't approve of."

"You have a gift for understatement, Father."

"He's an actor," Tony said. "Pat met him in Musket Beach, on the coast, where we have a little cabin."

"And he's one of the worst of the 'Hollywood actor-types,'" Pat said. "Thinks he's God's gift to women."

Tony motioned to the priest to tee off first. Father Mac bent over the chewed-up turf, teed up his ball, and straightened. "Well, I certainly hope that your trip to England won't be ruined by this—how did you describe him?"

Pat said quickly, "He's a genuine pain in the—" She stopped and glanced at Tony, an embarrassed expression on her pink face.

''Nave,'' said Father Mac, addressing his ball. ''You may say that he's a pain in the nave. Don't tell me that he's a pain in the apse.''

His drive went straight down the middle.

HOUSTON IN THE REARVIEW MIRROR

First Time in Paperback

A MILT KOVAK MYSTERY

SUSAN ROGERS COOPER

Milt Kovak doesn't believe for an instant that his sister shot her cheating husband and then tried to kill herself. And when the country sheriff goes after the bad guys in the big city, not one, but three attempts on his life prove him absolutely right....

"Chief Deputy Milt Kovak is a competent, low-key, really nice guy devoid of heroics and committed to getting to the truth."
—*Washington Post Book*

POISON PEN

A CHARLOTTE KENT MYSTERY

MARY KITTREDGE

Struggling each month to fill the pages of her new magazine for writers, Charlotte Kemp finds herself up the proverbial creek when she discovers her biggest, and very nearly only, contributor, Wesley Bell, sitting dead in her office swivel chair.

Then Charlotte discovers the hard way that she's at the top of somebody's must-kill list—an ending she'd like to skip entirely . . . if possible.

BARBARA PAUL

IN-LAWS AND OUTLAWS

Gillian Clifford, once a Decker in-law, returns to the family fold to comfort Raymond's widow, Connie. Clearly, the family is worried. Who hates the Deckers enough to kill them?

And as the truth behind the murder becomes shockingly clear, Gillian realizes that once a Decker, always a Decker—a position she's discovering can be most precarious indeed.

OTHER PEOPLE'S HOUSES

SUSAN ROGERS COOPER

In Prophesy County, Oklahoma, the unlikely event of a homicide is coupled with the likely event that if one occurs, the victim is somebody everybody knows....

And everybody knows nice bank teller Lois Bell who, along with her husband and three kids, dies of accidental carbon monoxide poisoning. But things just aren't sitting right with chief deputy Milton Kovak. Why were the victims' backgrounds completely untraceable? And why was the federal government butting its nose in the case?

"Milt Kovak tells his story with a voice that's as comforting as a rocking chair and as salty as a fisherman."

—*Houston Chronicle*

D · A · T · E

WITH A DEAD

D O C T O R

T O N I · B R I L L

Midge Cohen's mother has fixed her up again. What would it hurt to meet this nice Jewish doctor, a urologist even, and give him a try, she insists.

But all Dr. Leon Skripnik wants from Midge, an erstwhile Russian scholar, is a translation of a letter he's received from the old country. To get rid of him she agrees to his request. The next morning, he's found dead.

"An engaging first novel. A warm, observant, breezy talent is evident here."

—*Kirkus Reviews*

 WORLDWIDE LIBRARY™